THE illmoor CHRONICLES

The Yowler Foul-up

DAVID LEE STONE

Hodder Children's Books

A division of Hodder Headline Limited

First published in Great Britain in 2004
by Hodder Children's Books

This paperback edition published 2005

A Catalogue record for this book is available
from the British Library

ISBN 0 340 87399 X

Typeset in NewBaskerville by Avon DataSet Ltd,
Bidford-on-Avon, Warwickshire

Printed and bound in Great Britain by Clays Ltd, St Ives plc

Hodder Children's Books
a division of Hodder Headline Ltd
338 Euston Road
London NW1 3BH

For my grandmother,
Doris Christina Stone

And my late grandfather,
David Stone

Selected Dramatis Personae
(ye cast of characters)

Barrowbird — A distant relative of the forest hornbill.

Bowlcock, Lord — First ruler of Dullitch (deceased).

Coldwell, Jed — A gravedigger.

Curfew, Raviss — A viscount; Lord of Dullitch.

Dafisful, Grab — A thief.

Edwy — A Yowler acolyte.

Fjin, Frowd — Pub landlord.

Halvn — An elf guard.

Hopkirk — Secretary to Duke Modeset.

Hopkirk, Flicka — Fogrise aide, daughter of Hopkirk.

Innkeeper — Owner of the Steeplejack Inn.

Lauris the Lark — A Yowler priestess.

Lopsalm — A Yowler curate.

Marshall, Pegrand — Manservant to Duke Modeset.

Mixer — A gnome.

Modeset, Vandre — A disgraced noble, former Duke of Dullitch.

Moors — A Yowler acolyte.

Muldoon, Wrickshaw — A sorcerer.

Obegarde, Jareth — A loftwing detective.

Quickstint, Jimmy — A thief turned gravedigger.

Sorrow, Alan — Dullitch Quartermaster.

Spires, Milquay — Secretary to Viscount Curfew.

Vrunak, Augustus — An inventor.

ILLMOOR

GRINSWOOD FOREST

LEGRASH

BEANSTALK

CHUDDERFORD

SNEEZE

RIVER WASHOUT

SHINBONE

LITTLE IRKESOME

SHINBONE
FOREST

SHADEWELL

CRUST

GLEAMING MOUNTAINS

DULLITCH

CARFAX JUNGLES

An extract from the memoirs of Vandre Modeset,
43rd Duke of Dullitch:

The lowest of the low. I was comparatively destitute. Exiled from Dullitch along with my personal manservant, Pegrand, I returned to my birthplace: the forest kingdom of Fogrise. There I was happily reunited with Hopkirk, elderly retainer of the Keep and my father's own secretary. Together with these loyal aides and Hopkirk's indomitable daughter, Flicka, I determined to restore the kingdom to the grandeur it had once enjoyed . . .

It was a time of brief happiness and, without the chaos of city duties, Pegrand and I grew to become good friends.

Little did I suspect that Fate was set to urinate on my doorstep once more. Just five months later, I lost my beloved ancestral home in a complicated and particularly ruthless game of Snap.

Now, we have been forced to sink to new depths of poverty, and the others are becoming increasingly despondent. However, I remain optimistic about the future; I'm certain that something will turn up soon . . .

Prologue

Morning sunlight flooded Illmoor.

In the south it bathed the Gleaming Mountains and the fifteen spires of Dullitch, city capital of the continent. In the north it infiltrated the sprawling forest of Grinswood, home to a variety of magic sects including the Dark Trinity.

The Dark Trinity was nothing more than a name, a pronouncement. The Druids which made up its order were not in the least given over to darkness, but had simply been tarred by their proximity to the black heart of the wood. They served and represented Jort, God of Animal Kinship, a hypocritical entity famously disgraced when the King of the Gods paid him a surprise visit and found his sitting room full of deer heads.

The order occupied Jort's Hand, a fortified manse in

the centre of the wood, and a place only marginally less attractive than the decrepit moss that clung to its walls. The spiral towers of Jort's Hand rose high above the forest roof, and had stood solid against the wrath of time and the onslaught of the area's changeable weather cycle. Only the skyward towers caught the sunlight, due to the unique way in which the trees huddled together and locked branches. This meant the forest floor was always dark, although occasionally a few strobes of daylight would slip through the net of foliage and illuminate a daffodil. The effect was rather less than ethereal.

The Dark Trinity seldom took an interest in local affairs and few could blame them, considering the area. It was difficult to preach forest lore to a tribe whose only encounters with the animal kingdom came as a result of hunger. Occasionally, when the goblins killed a goat, or the trolls ambushed a wolf pack, the Dark Trinity would be called upon to intervene. These were sad and desperate times, and too many species were dwindling into extinction. Chief among these was the group of giant lizards known locally as the Batchtiki.

The Batchtiki, although unspeakably rare, were not worth much to anybody; their skins were rough and uncomfortable to wear, and their one talent relied heavily upon them being alive to perform it. Therefore, when a forest interloper (at no small risk to his health) was observed stealing a group of baby lizards from their nest in the north-eastern corner of the forest, the Dark Trinity were immediately concerned. However, being of sound mind, and suspecting, quite correctly, that this intruder was merely a pawn for some higher intelligence, they dispatched a barrowbird, one cursed to remain forever in the service of Jort, to spy for them and to trace the theft to its source . . .

The bird's mission, unbeknownst to the order at that time, would end in the cobbled streets of Dullitch, almost an entire continent away. It would begin . . .

Part One

The Great Returning

One

. . . Somewhere in the north-eastern corner of the forest, a tiny sprite emerged from the gloomy depths of a tree hollow and listened, translucent wings fluttering in the mid-morning breeze. A boot crushed it into the wood.

The thief was out of breath. He had run the length of Grinswood in just under three hours, which was a boastful feat for a man on horseback, let alone one with three broken toes, a limp and advanced constipation. He staggered, muttered a few obscenities and collapsed in a final wave of exhaustion, dropping his prize beside him. The sack wriggled as it hit the floor, and continued to do so for several minutes. Then it seemed to give up. The rest of the glade was still, with only the thief's heaving chest and slow, determined breaths punctuating the silence.

Time passed . . .

Presently, a barrowbird flew into the glade, landing on the gnarled lower branches of an ancient oak. It put its head on one side and considered the scene.

The thief, whose distinguishing features included one mechanical arm and a moon-shaped scar dissecting his chin, struggled to raise a charred eyebrow. The commotion inside the sack had started up again, and even appeared to be building; yet he took no notice.

Still, the bird watched.

A few minutes later, the thief had taken to rolling around on the grass in a number of failed attempts to get to his feet. Finally, he made a desperate lunge at the oak, twisted around and shouldered himself up. Blood rushed in his head as he fought to maintain his balance.

The barrowbird, totally nonplussed by the sudden display of energy, fixed its beady eyes on the sack.

Grinswood had become eerily silent. Shadows merged, and the trees seemed to move with them.

The thief took one last look around.

'Time to move,' he muttered, snatching up the sack and urging himself into a run.

When he'd disappeared from view, the barrowbird twitched and ruffled its feathers. Then it flew up on to a higher branch and cast a glance down the forest path, where a trail of disturbed foliage marked the thief's progress.

I'll take my time, it thought. This one looks like he's come a long way.

Two

For the specific attention of Duke Vandre Modeset,
Fourth Kennel Along,
Fechit's Dog Sanctuary,
Fogrise.

Dearest Cousin,

I was delighted to hear from the redoubtable Pagrind that you
have decided to accept my offer of hospitality. It has been some
months since the terms of your exile entitled you to return to
Dullitch, albeit as a citizen! I can assure you that the 'Rat
Catastrophe' is a long-forgotten piece of Dullitch history; people
have moved on! I do so look forward to seeing you and, to this
end, have taken the liberty of booking you four rooms at the
Steeplejack Inn, a grand boarding house on Royal Road. I

*trust your visit, along with that of your staff, will be both
enjoyable and relaxing.*

Regards,
Your cousin,
Raviss Curfew, VISCOUNT, LORD OF DULLITCH

Duke Modeset had read the letter many times, and
was still of the opinion that it had been written by one of
the palace's many scribes. As far as he was concerned,
anyone who described Pegrand as 'redoubtable' probably
didn't have a royal bone in their body. He could only
imagine the pleasure Curfew's minions would have taken
from reading the address; it must have provided them
with no end of amusement to learn that he'd been living
in a dog's home. Thank the gods they didn't know he'd
been sharing . . .

He sighed, folded the letter neatly in two and looked
around for somewhere to file it. His gaze eventually
came to rest on something that he assumed was
supposed to be a bureau. A curious piece of furniture,
it looked as if the carpenter responsible had started out
with high hopes but had evidently been sidetracked en
route to perfection. Modeset reached down to open the
drawer and scowled as the handle broke off. Shoddy.
Oh well, at least the place felt like home. He tried and
failed to replace the handle three times before letting it
fall to the floor, where it clattered noisily on the wooden

boards. He propped the parchment on the windowsill instead.

Despite the cracked plaster and crumbling beams, there could be little doubt that the Steeplejack Inn was indeed a five-star resort, the only problem being that a five-star resort in Dullitch was the equivalent of a mutant cesspool anywhere else on the continent. Modeset wasn't sure of the minimum requirements for these classifications, but the Spittle Bridge had three stars and there was water under *that*.

Modeset crossed to the bed, turned and let himself fall back on to it. The explosion of sound was like a dwarf war-hammer hitting a wardrobe door. Pain ricocheted through his back and he sat up with a start. His eyes bulged.

A moment later, the duke's faithful manservant erupted through the bedroom door. His face was redder than a beetroot, and he was clearly out of breath from his bolt along the landing.

'You all right, milord?' he wheezed, leaning against the door frame for support.

The duke, still grasping his back, glared at him.

'Only, did you hear that almighty bang?'

Modeset nodded.

'So did we. What was it, d'you reckon?'

'It was me, Pegrand,' Modeset managed, suppressing a groan. 'Go and tell the Innkeeper that I want another bed. This mattress is thinner than your anorexic aunt.'

'I'll have a word in his ear, milord.'

'Good man. Where's your room?'

Pegrand pointed skyward.

''Snot exactly Marble Heights, though,' he confided, lowering his voice to a whisper. 'There's a big leak in the roof: the Innkeeper says it doesn't let much in, but I've been speaking to a few of the guests and they reckon the last bloke who stopped in the attic drowned. I dunno how the others're getting on.'

Modeset put his head in his hands, and tried to focus on the positives. Firstly, he was on holiday. That, generally speaking, was a good thing. He was accompanied by a full complement of personal staff, which was another. Negatively speaking, the Inn was a dump, the city a nightmare he'd spent the best part of five years trying to forget, and the staff a pair of depraved cultural drop-outs from a depressing backwater he couldn't wait to forget. Then there was Pegrand. He imagined a series of public humiliations and disastrous misunderstandings festering on the horizon, and determined to escape before they arrived. After all, Fate was avoidable; it was destiny that caused you all the trouble.

Three

Modeset checked his pocket watch. There was still half an hour to go before dinner. Having already paced back and forth in his room for what seemed like a millennium, Modeset decided to take a nap. He carefully lowered himself on to the bed, worked his body into a halfway comfortable position and tried to drift off.

CRASH!

His eyes flicked open, and he sat bolt upright.

The inward shutters were devastated; one had been wrenched off its hinges and the other had slammed into the far wall with such velocity that it had spawned a network of cracks in the plaster.

For a moment the duke observed the rules of stunned silence, and remained absolutely still. Then he leapt off the bed and hurried over to the window.

The street below was dark and shadowy, and the bleak light offered by the lamp wicks betrayed no obvious signs of an explosion.

And so it begins, he thought bitterly. *Word of my arrival has got around and suddenly everyone's out wandering the streets with a brick in each hand. Ha! So much for moving on!*

He peered cautiously out of the window, expecting at any second to be bombarded by the rest of someone's garden wall.

Nothing; the street was empty. Silence reigned. From what he could make out, the rest of Royal Road's crooked buildings were largely undisturbed. There was a fire blazing somewhere to the north, but nothing to account for the sudden, meteoric destruction of the shutters.

Modeset sighed, and pulled the outer set closed. He was about to return to bed when he saw the rock on the floor beside the bureau. It was wrapped in parchment which, in turn, was fastened with string. For a moment he just stared at the rock as if waiting for it to sprout legs and run under the door.

Then he sighed despondently, bent down and tried to pick it up, groaning when it turned out to be a stone heavier than the average cannon ball.

Puffing and panting with the effort, he hefted the rock on to the bed, untied the string and folded out the parchment. There was a note on the back.

Modeset squinted at the writing, which was crude and

betrayed a certain loathing for punctuation. It certainly wasn't what he expected:

TONIGHT WAS A TASTER THERE IS MORE TO COME STAY AWAY FROM WAREHOUSE SIX IF YOU DON'T YOU WILL WAKE UP FEELING NOT VERY WELL WITH A CROSSBOW BOLT IN YOUR BACK YOU HAVE BEEN WARNED THERE ARE MANY TORTURE INSTRUMENTS WHICH WE ARE NOT AFRAID TO USE IN AN EMERGENCY AND WE KNOW YOU'RE A LOFTWING BECAUSE YOU ONLY FOLLOW AT NIGHT AND WE HAVE LOTS OF SILVER WHICH KILLS YOU LOT SO BE WARNED AND NO MORE OUT OF YOU AFTER THAT THEN.

MISTER X (AND THAT'S NOT MY REAL NAME SO DON'T THINK YOU'VE GOT ME THERE).

Modeset looked from the rock to the note and back again, his attention finally diverting to the window. The remaining inward shutter broke off from its hinge and crashed on to the floorboards. He was about to hide it under the bed when there was a heavy-handed knock on the bedroom door.

'Milord?'

Modeset started, thrust the parchment under his pillow and pulled the bedcovers over the cannon-ball rock.

'Yes?' he shouted, testily. 'What is it, Pegrand?'

'Dinner's in five minutes, milord. Thought you might

like a quick reminder. Also, Flicka wanted me to tell you that she's boarded Vicious at a local place called the Stays. She said it might cost a bit more than the two crowns a night we were quoted, because he'd already bitten the bloke twice by the time she'd signed the register.'

'Mmm? Oh, yes. Thank you.'

'No problem. Just yell if you need anything else.'

'Good show. I'll be along presently.'

'Okay, milord. No worries, then. Everything all right in there, is it? Only, I thought I heard a noise.'

'Yes, that was me, Pegrand. I . . . tried to close the wardrobe.'

'You've got a wardrobe in there now, milord? That's a result.'

Modeset looked around frantically.

'No!' he yelled. 'It . . . fell out of the window, I'm afraid. Look, I'll be out in a few moments.'

'Right you are, milord.'

When the manservant's footsteps had dissipated, Modeset snaked a hand under the pillow and retrieved the parchment. After a second reading, he rolled it up and stowed it away inside his tunic. He had a funny feeling that it was going to be one of those nights.

Four

Elsewhere.

From the state of the room you could tell it was part of a hovel in one of the seedier parts of the city. The furniture was threadbare, the walls collapsing, and a dynasty of cockroaches fought terrible wars beneath the floorboards. Its occupant, a gnome with brass teeth and a network of terrible scars, was studying something of great importance.

The book stood open on the table. It was a heavy tome, more than five times the size of a regular book, and its pages were inked with bold script and elaborate illustrations. The turning of each leaf was accompanied by a dull cackle, and the gnome spent several moments smoothing the pages down so that the book would close properly. It had to close properly. Otherwise it wouldn't fit the gap in the wall, and some filthy thief would sneak in and steal it. Such was the norm in Dullitch. Eventually, when the Ultimate Goal was achieved, he'd move somewhere smaller. Still, that was a long way off, and many parts of the Mistress's plan still needed to be realized. Nobody had heard from the lizard thief, yet, and he'd been gone for weeks! Oh well ... that was definitely not his problem.

The gnome closed the book and stowed it away in the wall, pulling the old, half-rotted dresser in front to conceal it. Then he returned to his little stool and gazed down at an area of the table containing an inkwell, a feathered quill and a box. This, he reflected, shouldn't be too difficult.

He was certain that Obegarde, the loftwing who'd been following him for two, maybe three days was either from or employed by the palace. Unfortunately, his research hadn't turned up much more than a name, but then an official palace employee wouldn't be shacked up at a coaching inn.

Hmm ... a freelance, then; some sort of investigator. He grimaced at the thought. This was disastrous! How could they possibly have found out? Mistress Lark had worked at the palace, but it wouldn't have been her, surely? She was much too smart, far too careful. Well, whatever, someone had let slip. Ha! And they'd had the nerve to call *him* stupid. All things considered, it was a miracle the group had managed to keep their little secret at all.

Still, the threat *should* suffice. He certainly hoped it would, because the loftwing was no minor irritant; if the creature found out enough to make a report, he had the potential to ruin everything. It just wasn't fair; he'd been so *careful*!

What to do, what to do . . .

First things first; the old inventor. Mistress Lark had been very definite about that; he knew too much and was the most immediate threat to the group. Besides, he was long past being useful; the machine was built and it wasn't likely to go wrong. Even so, assassination was a little harsh; perhaps he should give the old boy a scare, instead. Then he might leave town of his own accord . . .

Muttering under his breath, the gnome took up the quill and, dipping it into the inkwell, began to write. Then he folded the parchment into segments, tore neatly along all the edges and placed a number of blank pieces inside the pockets of a dark cloak he'd collected, keeping hold of the original piece he'd written on. Then he took the quill *and* its grimy inkwell.

There, he thought, that's just about everything.

Fastening his cloak about him, the gnome hurried from the hovel. It was going to be a busy night . . .

Five

When Modeset reached the first-floor landing, most of his staff were already out in force.

Pegrand was dressed in the standard leather britches and scruffy doublet he always wore, hair spilling out from behind his ears while managing to avoid the top of his head completely. Flicka, Hopkirk's daughter and the only member of Modeset's staff still enjoying her twenties, had settled for a pure white robe that made her look more like a druid sacrifice than a royal aide. Her long dark hair, pale skin and delicate elfin features were somewhat marred by the quizzical expression which had camped on her face since the day she was born.

The two of them constituted quite a picture. Modeset didn't think much of the presentation, but then, judging by their collective stare, they were just as disgusted by his choice of formal dress. He couldn't for the life of him understand why; the armoured suit might be old, but at least it wasn't paid for.

'Now, this evening represents my first experience of Dullitch hospitality for some time,' he said. 'I want everyone to make a conscious effort, and that includes you, Pegrand.'

'Yes, milord. Got some impressive jokes lined up for the after-dinner discussions.'

'None of your sledgehammer wit, please.'

'No, milord. Right you are, then. I'll keep a zip on the monkey gag until the crockery's collected. Do we know how many other guests are coming?'

'Not many, I fear. It's just us, the landlord and, supposedly, one other gentleman. We're getting special treatment by order of the throne. As I understood it, most of the guests are confined to their rooms until after the meal.'

'Should be OK, then, as long as they don't try to dig themselves out. Who's the jailer?'

'I don't find that even remotely amusing, Pegrand.'

'Sorry, milord.'

'And how about you, Flicka?' said Modeset. 'All ready for your first dinner in Dullitch?'

Hopkirk's daughter swept back a lock of her long, ebony hair and fixed Modeset with her sparkly blue eyes.

'Do I have any choice?' she said.

'Splendid! Where's your father?'

21

'Sleeping; he's still upset that you lost the Keep to those card sharks. In fact, he's threatening to sleep through the entire visi—'

'Good, good,' Modeset beamed, ignoring the accusation. They weren't a bad lot, he had to admit; Pegrand might have his bad days, Flicka tended to look down her nose at anyone who didn't have a knighthood and her father rarely mustered enough energy to raise an eyelid but, all in all, he could've done a lot worse.

'We'll descend the stairs in single file, ladies first,' he said. 'That's you, Flicka, just in case there's any doubt. I noticed Pegrand took a step forward then and, while he undoubtedly has the tongue of a washerwoman, he is by no means a lady.'

Flicka rolled her eyes and took to the stairs.

'Mind your head on that candelabrum as you go,' the duke called out. 'Very tasteful, isn't it?'

'Milord?'

'Yes, OK, Pegrand. Down you go, then. Be sure to announce me as soon as you get to the dining hall ... and no silly voices this time, I implore you.'

Six

Augustus Vrunak had just climbed into bed when the doorbell clanged. Nobody else in Dullitch would have had such bad luck, he thought bitterly. And he was right; nobody else in Dullitch had a doorbell. Such was the price of being an inventor in a city that never sleeps. He'd rigged up the device on a rope-pulley system that ran from the entrance door of his cottage to a bracket above his bedroom door.

He grimaced, swore under his breath and waited for the small brass tinkle to subside.

Clank, clink, clink, clink;

Clank, clink, clink;

Clank, clink;

CLANG, clank, clink, clink, clink.

Augustus scowled. Whoever it was, they obviously had

no intention of waiting until the morning to see him. He climbed out of bed, padded over to the window in his carpet slippers and peered out at the front lawn. Unusual; his mystery visitor had closed the gate after him. Perhaps it was his sister. She'd spent most of the evening having dinner with him and he supposed she might have forgotten something.

CLANG, clank, clink, clink.

'OK, for goodness' sake!' Augustus bellowed. 'I'm coming.'

He pulled a dressing gown over his nightshirt and went downstairs, muttering under his breath. On the way down, he glanced into his stairway mirror and reflected, rather bitterly, that he was beginning to look like a chubby old walrus. Oh, well, age tended to do that to you . . .

Odd; the front door was stuck.

He put all his weight behind his heels and leaned back, but the door just wouldn't budge. He spat on his hands and tried again, then put one foot against the frame and heaved with all his might. Nothing happened. Either damp had expanded the wood in a ludicrously short space of time or – he hesitated to think of an alternative – or somebody else was pulling from the other side.

The brass bell clanged again and Augustus suddenly felt extremely cold and alone.

'Is there anybody there?' he called.

He looked down. A small square of paper had been pushed underneath the door. There was writing on it.

He reached down carefully and picked it up, one eye on the door in case an axe head came through it.

The paper was perfectly cut, an exact rectangle. He read:

STAND AWAY FROM THE DOOR AUGUSTUS WE HAVE HOLD OF IT

His mind raced. The Yowler? It had to be; they were the only ones with a reason.

Sweat began to form on the inventor's brow and he found himself shivering.

'What do you want from me?' he called.

A second sheet was slipped on to the mat. Augustus read:

DO NOT ATTEMPT TO MAKE A BREAK FOR THE BACK DOOR EITHER WE ARE THERE ALSO AND WILL KILL YOU ON SIGHT

'But why? I haven't done anything wrong!'

He bent down to retrieve the answer. Were they attempting to get to him through his arthritis?

YOU HAVE BEEN TALKING HAVEN'T YOU TALKING TO AN ENEMY OF THE GROUP

He stood back, thrust his hands into his robe pockets and swallowed.

'No,' he said. 'I never!'

BE VERY CAREFUL HOW YOU ANSWER AUGUSTUS

'There's no need for that kind of talk. I'm already afraid.'

YOU SHOULD BE LISTENING WITH INTENT

TOMORROW MORNING YOU WILL PACK YOUR THINGS AND LEAVE DULLITCH DESTROY ANY REMAINING EVIDENCE OF YOUR UNION WITH US BEFORE YOU DEPART PLACE YOUR FRONT-DOOR KEY UNDER THE FLOWERPOT

Augustus put his head on one side.

'I don't have a flowerpot,' he said.

There was a brief pause before the note appeared.

A FLOWERPOT WILL BE PROVIDED

'Do I get a plant with it?'

YOU ARE SKATING ON VERY THIN ICE AUGUSTUS

'Sorry; didn't mean any disrespect. Go on.'

UNDERSTAND THAT AFTER TONIGHT YOU MUST NEVER SPEAK OF THIS EVENT UNTIL THE DAY YOU DIE

Augustus gave this a moment's thought.

'When will that be?' he asked.

WHENEVER YOU DECIDE TO SPEAK OF THIS EVENT

'Ah,' said the inventor. 'Now I'm getting you.' He pulled his robe tight around him and leaned against the door of his broom closet.

HAVE WE ESTABLISHED A MUTUAL TRUST DO YOU THINK

'Yes. I'll do as you say.'

YOU ARE A SENSIBLE MAN AUGUSTUS VRUNAK

Time passed. At length, the inventor put one ear to the door.

'You still there?' he called.

Silence.

He turned the handle and cautiously peered out into the night. The garden was empty. It showed no sign of having been disturbed, apart from the rusty gate that swung loose in the wind.

$\mathcal{S}e\mathcal{N}en$

The grand dinner to welcome the return of Duke Modeset began badly and looked like going downhill from there. The Innkeeper, a stout man of indefinite age, was unfathomably moody. He mumbled recognizable obscenities under his breath, and slammed the dishes down with such fervour that they almost bounced. Moreover, he didn't bother to introduce the other guest, who arrived late and chose a seat so far from the party that they could only communicate with him by sign language.

Eventually, after a number of ignored questions and a few embarrassed silences, they managed to discover the root of the Innkeeper's anxiety. It turned out that, despite a promised advance from Viscount Curfew, he had yet to be paid for the party's stay. The duke spent some time assuring him that the bills would be settled, but he seemed totally disgusted with the group, sneering every time one of them reached for a plate. Modeset fancied that the only thing keeping the Innkeeper from turfing the group on to the streets was a fear of reprisal from the crown. Consequently, a very uncomfortable meal ensued.

'Um, I say, isn't this nice?' Modeset lied. 'It's been so long since I've sampled the delicacies of capital cuisine! As I was saying to Flicka, here, I really should get out and see the city again; I've almost forgotten what it looks like! She's young, of course, probably wouldn't be interested in culture. I doubt if the palace would make the Flicka list of places to see! Hahaha!'

'The palace!' muttered the Innkeeper. 'Now there's an idea. Why don't you all go and stay *there*?'

'I'm interested in culture if it involves magic,' said Flicka, bringing a dark veil of silence over the table. 'I've always been interested in that. In fact, Father got me this spellbook in Spittle. It's only theory, of course, but I've learned a lot.'

'Are you interested in anything *else*, Flicka?' Modeset prompted, trying to drag the subject away from illegalities. 'After all, Dullitch is a very big pla—'

'As a matter of fact I am, Lord M. What about the Yowlers? It amazes me how a city can function with a criminally insane cult thriving beneath it.'

'Yes, well, enough of—'

'I mean,' she went on. 'Apart from the forgers at

Counterfeit House, I understand there's something called the Rooftop Runners, is that right? Thieves and the like, aren't they?'

'I'd really rather we didn't talk about it,' Modeset snapped. 'Besides, the Yowlers were born out of an obscure religion and religion has always been a dicey subject here in Dullitch. I recall a time, not so long ago, when virgins not much older than yourself were chained to rocks and sacrificed for the greater glory of some bizarre god.'

'I reckon you might be thinkin' o' druidics, there, milord,' said Pegrand.

'No,' Flicka interrupted. 'That's definitely how the Yowlers started—

'I'm telling you, it was—'

An argument ensued.

Modeset, practically unconscious with boredom, tried to relieve the monotony by watching the stranger at the far end of the table devouring a salad. The man appeared to be having terrible trouble with his meal, spitting out every mouthful of lettuce mere seconds after forking it in. There's a fellow with a few problems, if I'm not mistaken, he thought. When the stranger looked up suddenly, Modeset returned his attention to the argument and was about to interrupt Pegrand's incessant banter, when a resounding boom from the far end of the table cut through the meal like a rogue scimitar.

'IS THERE GARLIC ON THIS?' it said.

30

The Innkeeper leaned around Pegrand to peer over at the stranger.

'Eh? What's that you're saying? Come over here, will you?'

The stranger lifted his plate and moved several places down the table, nodded and muttered 'Evening' at everyone as he took a new seat. He was thickset but looked incredibly sharp; he was also covered in cuts and bruises.

'I said,' he began, eyeing the Innkeeper dubiously, 'did you put garlic on this salad?'

The Innkeeper nodded.

'A bit, for the flavour; sorry, I forgot.'

'Oh, right. Can I have some of this chicken instead, or is there garlic on everything?'

'Chicken's fine; fresh from the oven.'

The stranger reached over to cut off a slice, and almost melted in the heat of Pegrand's stare.

I reckon you must be a vampire, it seemed to say.

He smiled pleasantly at the manservant, cursing his own ability to read thoughts at close range. He wondered if, just once, it might work both ways. *Why don't you stuff off and die, you filthy, stinking little piece of excrement?*

Pegrand's continued grin indicated that his own ability to read thoughts was still a long way off.

'Yes, I am,' the stranger said, instead. 'Part vampire, on my mother's side, which unfortunately means I've just the one fang, I only drink blood when there's no wine going and I can't sleep a wink past midnight. The name's Obegarde. Delighted, I'm sure.'

Apart from the Innkeeper, who continued to scowl at the empty spaces on the meat tray, every face at the table took on a kind of blank, isolated stare.

Fantastic, thought Modeset. Not only am I living on promised means at a five-star hotel with holes in the roof, and not only am I the mistaken target for some rock-throwing lunatic with a grudge, *now* I'm having dinner with a vampire.

'If it bothers you, I'll go back and sit over there,' said Obegarde, pointing towards the far end of the table.

'N-no, nonsense, er, wouldn't hear of it,' said the duke. 'This here is Pegrand, my manservant, and Flicka Hopkirk, my secretary's somewhat *argumentative* daughter. I'm—'

'Modeset,' Obegarde interrupted. 'Yes, I remember your reign very well. Lot of rats about, I recall.'

'Yes, well, have some wine, and a few of those grapes. Make yourself welcome.'

'Thank you,' said Obegarde, trying as hard as everyone else to ignore the Innkeeper's incessant mumbling.

'I wasn't sure I'd be welcome,' Obegarde continued, 'some people can be a little hostile.'

'Doesn't bother me,' Pegrand cut in. 'Part undead on your mother's side, you say? Isn't there a name for that? Lowdown or somethin' similar?'

Here we go, thought Modeset. Now he's going to get us all killed.

'I assume the name you're thinking of is "loftwing",' Obegarde replied, taking up the wine bottle and emptying it into a clean glass. 'But it's a spiteful word and I don't find it very flattering. Besides, we don't have much in common with the dark breed; all of the longevity and none of the class, so to speak.'

Modeset had practically turned to stone. His thoughts raced to the rolled parchment still concealed in his tunic. So that's who the note was meant for, he thought. Whoever threw the rock must have intended it for the vampire and thrown it through the wrong window. Interesting.

Pegrand sniffed and nodded.

'Must be a borin' old stretch for you lot,' he said. 'Moochin' through a hundred lifetimes in the darkness while the rest of us peg out. What do you do with yourself?'

Obegarde, who'd been looking sideways at Modeset with a curious expression on his face, gave the manservant a sudden, impassive smile.

'I'm an investigator,' he said. 'I specialize in looking for people who don't want to be found.'

A number of eyebrows were raised.

'How d'you know?' said Pegrand.

'Mmm?'

'Well, these people you're looking for. How d'you know they don't want to be found?'

The vampire considered this.

'Well,' he said eventually. 'It's obvious, isn't it? I can't find them easily.'

'Yeah, but that could just be you.'

'Haha! Yes, I suppose it could. No, in fact, it's just a polite way of saying that my job involves a lot of confrontation.'

'Ah, I see,' said Pegrand. 'That explains why you look like you just spent an hour in a dustbin full o' kittens.'

Kill him, thought Modeset. Please, do us all a favour. Leap across the table and rip his throat out.

Obegarde smiled, but said nothing.

'I'm sure Mr Obegarde would rather not discuss his business at the dinner table,' Modeset interrupted, glaring with intensity when he saw the look on Pegrand's face. 'Client confidentiality, and all that.'

There was a general murmur of agreement, and a few smaller pockets of conversation rippled between the staff and the Innkeeper.

Eventually, the Innkeeper struggled to his feet and shuffled off towards the kitchens. Modeset made a gesture for Pegrand to follow suit, but the manservant had nodded off. Flicka collected the crockery instead. The atmosphere, which had been hovering over the table like a big black cloud, finally lifted.

'Sooooo,' said Obegarde, prolonging the word until everyone still conscious was out of earshot. 'Where is it, then? This message that was so obviously meant for me?'

Modeset frowned.

'I've absolutely no idea what you're talking about,' he said.

'Oh don't bother with all that rubbish,' snapped Obegarde. 'I read your mind.'

There was a moment of silence.

'Very well,' said the duke, keeping one eye on the little wooden door to the kitchens. He put a hand inside his tunic and produced the roll of parchment.

Obegarde snatched it from him.

'Good,' he said. 'Now, I'd appreciate it if you forgot the contents.'

He finished chewing on his chicken leg and tossed it on to a plate heaped high with leftovers.

Modeset shrugged.

'I confess I'm quite intrigued,' he said. 'It doesn't sound as if the chap's too interested in talking.'

Obegarde got to his feet. Modeset was surprised at the size of the man. Somehow, you expected vampires to be thin and gaunt. Obegarde looked like an athletic ogre.

'There's more to it than that,' he said. 'And, with respect, none of it's any of your business, your *lordship*.'

Modeset was slow to nod.

'Nice to have met you,' said Obegarde. He stood, returned to his original seat and pulled on his overcoat. 'Thank Grumpy for the meal, will you?'

He turned and swept from the room, coat-tails billowing out behind him.

Modeset watched the vampire go, and swallowed. Betrayed by my own mind, he thought. Whatever next?

'Mmmff, Morris! Where's the cauldron?' said a voice. Pegrand woke with a ghoulish yawn and stared about him with sudden panic. 'What? Where'd I go?'

'You drifted off, Pegrand,' said Modeset, finishing his wine. 'Happens to the best of us.'

The manservant managed a lop-sided grin.

'Ah, sorry about that, milord,' he said. 'Did I miss much?'

'Nothing,' the duke replied, lowering his wineglass on to the table top. 'Nothing at all.'

Eight

Mist was descending on the streets of Dullitch, swirling around the ancient lamp-posts and lending a mysterious haze to the normality of midnight. In the cemetery, a light flickered between the gravestones, becoming more and more erratic as the wind began to pick up. Someone was digging.

Jimmy Quickstint scooped up a generous pile of earth with his rusty spade, struggling to keep the tool level while countless grains poured over the sides in a filthy brown avalanche. Then, employing a deft flick of the wrist, he spun the spade one hundred and eighty degrees, depositing the dirt on a growing pile beside the plot. An old weather-beaten lamp perched jauntily over the grave.

Several scoops later, gasping with a mixture of relief and exhaustion, he drove the spade hard into the dirt, embedding it in the soil so deeply that it remained upright. He mopped his sweating brow with the sleeve of his overalls and looked up at his superior.

The old man was sitting on the grassy bank nearby, filling a dingy brown pipe with small shags of rough tobacco. He went through this same routine every night, as regular as clockwork. It was one of the man's many habits that drove his apprentice insane; that and the fact that he never actually seemed to do any work.

'Finished,' Jimmy called over the lip of the open grave.

'Aye,' came the short reply.

'Should I climb out now?'

'Aye.'

'Should I drown in a pool of my own blood?'

'Aye.'

Jimmy rolled his eyes and, after a number of unsuccessful attempts, managed to struggle out of the hole and roll on to level ground.

The old man finished binding the seal of his tobacco pouch with string and stowed it safely away in the confines of his grubby overcoat. Finally he seemed to notice his apprentice crouching on the ground before him, gasping for breath by the lungful.

' 'Ave you reached ol' Clifford?' the old man asked, scratching the fast-receding hair beneath his flat cap. 'If you have, you've gone too far.'

Jimmy looked about him in bewilderment.

'Come again?' he managed.

'I said, 'ave you reached old Clifford?'

'Who's Clifford?'

'Him what's buried down that there hole.'

'No, sir. *This* is the grave for Mr Flunk, due in tomorrow. Remember?'

'Aye, and that's as maybe, lad, but that there plot is already occupied. You don't want to go too far down.'

Jimmy looked back into the open grave from which he'd just emerged and shook his head in amazement.

'You mean there's someone already down there?' he gasped.

'Aye,' the old man confirmed. ''As been these last fifty year or so.'

'But, but what about Mr Flunk? The priests told his family he could go in here!'

'Aye, I know. That's why we can't go down as far as Clifford, see?'

Jimmy swallowed, struggling against the odds to force back the horror of the situation. 'How long has this been going on?' he said.

The old man put his head on one side.

'Oh, we ran outta room down here a long while back.'

'How long? My uncle was buried in this cemetery!'

The old man waved him down in an attempt to restore calm. 'Now don't you fret none, young'un, your uncle's prob'ly still a restin' right where you left him.' He sucked in his scraggly lower lip. 'An' happen when was that?'

'About ten years ago,' said Jimmy, tapping his foot impatiently.

'Ooh, now le' me see, right around the time of – yes, I 'spect he's a few down by now but he'll be there, right enough.'

'A few down? A FEW DOWN?' Jimmy screamed, marching off towards the cemetery gates. 'That's it! I'm out of here; you can find yourself another damn slave!'

Nine

Morning arrived, another murky one.

Apart from the Diamond Clock Tower on Crest Hill, Dullitch Palace was easily the largest and most impressively placed structure in the city. The building itself was falling to pieces, though, on a superficial glance from the gates, it retained much of its original grace and beauty (something that, sadly, couldn't be said of the guards).

'What do you mean "He doesn't want to see me"?' Modeset exclaimed. 'I'm his cousin, for goodness' sake, I'm here at his request! I'm royalty!'

'The viscount is busy with matters of state,' said the sentry, an ageing, thickset elf with crooked teeth and more scars than the tooth fairy (the citizens of Dullitch didn't like to let go of *anything*).

'He's not seeing anyone until the trade war with Legrash is sorted out.'

'There is no trade war between Legrash and Dullitch!' the duke snapped. 'It's just an excuse you use to fob off the citizens, and I know that because I invented it! I demand entrance now!'

The duke made a move to step past the guard and found his way barred by a heavy iron pike.

'What's this?' Modeset demanded. 'A peasant uprising?'

'I ain't no peasant,' said the guard. 'And the only uprising round here's likely to involve you on the end of this.'

He indicated the pike head and widened his grin. 'Some of us haven't forgot the last time you occupied the palace,' he added. Modeset took a step back, shouldering Pegrand aside in the process.

'Don't let 'em talk to you like that, Lord M!' yelled Flicka, nudging the duke forward with a bemused smile on her face. She'd followed the dynamic duo around the city for the best part of a morning and was now thoroughly sick and tired of the duke's attitude. As far as she could see, it was no use looking down on people who weren't looking up.

Modeset, however, was thinking along the same lines. So far, he'd received the type of hospitality usually reserved for barbarian invaders. What happened to people forgiving and forgetting? At the very least he'd expected a fanfare at Modeset's Fort, a guardhouse originally opened in his honour. As it was, the party had to hammer on the door and throw stones at the windows for well over half an hour, before an oily lieutenant had emerged like primordial man into the light to play the Modeset family anthem on his nose-flute. Eventually, after a lot of arguing they'd managed to wrangle three cups of tea and a biscuit. Some Royal Visit; he might as well have taken a tip out of Hopkirk's book and stayed in bed.

The palace was the final straw; Modeset was beginning to lose patience.

'Pegrand,' he said. 'You're supposed to be trained in self-defence, aren't you? Teach this insolent fool a lesson he'll never forget!'

The manservant, who'd been retrieving part of the guardhouse biscuit from his teeth with a grimy fingernail, looked suddenly taken aback.

'I can't use self-defence unless I'm bein' attacked, milord,' he said sheepishly.

Modeset looked totally astounded.

'Don't be ridiculous, man!' he said. 'You have to bring pre-emptive measures into play, don't you see? Provoke the situation! The only way you're ever going to need something like self-defence is if the aggressor comes straight at you, and the only way to ensure that, is by hitting him first; like this!'

The duke sprang forward and glanced a blow off the guard's chin. Although lightweight, it caught the elf completely by surprise and he flew back, knocking into the portcullis control mechanism. Guards ran in every direction, displaying the sudden panic of men who'd been prepared for mass invasion for so long, they'd actually forgotten what to do in the light of any minor trouble.

The portcullis slammed down.

Then the guards stopped running and looked around them.

Two blurred shapes were fast receding over the newly erected Gatehouse Bridge. The guards looked at one another, and then they were gone, kicking up dust behind them.

Flicka watched the chase until all had disappeared into Palace Street, then she began to follow at a leisurely pace.

Ten

Modeset had never run so fast in his life.

Heart pounding, arms pumping and limbs screaming in submission, he raced along Palace Street as if the entire Dullitch Army was after him. He couldn't think, he couldn't hear and, thanks to the wind, he could only see faint blurs through the watery haze of his tears. More importantly, though, he was seriously beginning to enjoy himself.

The pair had been together up until the junction with Royal Road. That's where he'd lost Pegrand. A backward glance had seen the manservant shin up an oak tree in the front garden of a rather elegant cottage.

Boots pounded the cobbles.

Modeset peered over his shoulder and saw that the elf guard he'd punched was leading the pursuit. The enraged, slightly dazed expression on its face suggested that its job description hadn't included taking physical abuse from down-on-their-luck members of the nobility.

The market was in full swing. Modeset made for a tightly packed group of spice stalls on the east side of the square.

On his way past the first stall he grabbed a bowl of blue dust and threw it wide. The bowl spun in the air, spewing an ocean curtain over the front line of guards and two orcish spice merchants, who just happened to be in the way. They waved their fists and shouted gruff obscenities at Modeset but, thankfully, in a dialect he didn't recognize.

Energy waning, the duke ran on, never daring to look behind him. He knew the elf was still in pursuit because of the rhythmic clanking noise its armour made as it ran. Modeset thought that it sounded like an elderly war-wagon about to give up the ghost. As if in answer to the thought, the clanking ceased. And the duke made a cardinal mistake: he slowed down and looked behind him.

The elf guard, having suddenly propelled itself into the air in a desperate, last-ditch attempt to catch up, brought Modeset down in a single striking movement.

They rolled over and over on the ground. Despite Modeset's frantic struggles, the guard clearly had the situation well under control. It leaped to its feet and dragged the duke up after it.

'You wanted to see the viscount, right?' it said. 'Well, *now* you've got your wish. You can see Lord Curfew immediately. In chains.'

The punch wasn't hard, but it caught Modeset completely unawares, and knocked him to the ground.

The guard muttered something under his breath and, hefting the duke on to one shoulder, headed back to the palace. On the way, he was stopped by a rather attractive young lady who asked him directions to the market square. He was in the process of describing an ideal route, when she suddenly brought her knee up between his legs, and caught him with a chop across the back of the neck as he dropped the duke. He didn't remember much after that.

Modeset woke up running. Still groggy from the elf's punch, he peered around to see Flicka running beside him, her arm wedged under his shoulder for support. He was about to congratulate her on the rescue when she suddenly propelled him through a shop doorway so fast that he hit the counter head first and almost knocked himself out again. She quickly hurried in after him and slammed the door, ducking down as a group of guards bolted past the window.

Modeset dug his fingernails into the counter and dragged himself to his feet. They were in a toyshop, and the watchword was *clutter*. Every shelf was packed with rocking horses, dollies, teddy bears and wooden soldiers.

The shopkeeper was so small that Modeset at first mistook him for one of the toys. He'd been walking along the counter when an arm shot out to greet him.

'Ah! Welcome to my shop. Would you like a teddy bear?'

Modeset declined the handshake.

'Not particularly.'

'How about a dolly for your daughter?'

'She's not my daughter and, no, thank you.'

'Wooden horse for the young lady?'

'We don't want anything,' Modeset snapped, still watching out for the militia.

'Then what did you come in here for?'

'We came in to get away from the guards,' said Flicka, stepping up to the counter.

'You're criminals then!' said the shopkeeper excitedly. 'I have just the thing!'

He disappeared behind a small curtain at the back of the shop, returning with his arms full.

'This is a magical dolly from Phlegm. Highly illegal and terribly dangerous in the wrong hands – it excretes acid, is highly inflammable, and also explodes in water.'

'That is the most despicable thing I've ever heard,' Modeset snapped, snatching the doll from the shopkeeper's outstretched arms and slamming it down on the counter. 'You sell life-threatening toys in this shop? During my reign, I'd have had you hanged for that.'

'Your reign? Oh goodness, yes. I thought I recognized you. We do stuffed rats, your lordship.'

'How amusing.'

'What does the teddy do?' asked Flicka, pointing to the small brown bear under the little man's other arm.

'Ah, now this is Sven, a very magical toy indeed, and not at all dangerous. In fact, if sorcery weren't banned in Dullitch, he'd be perfectly legal. Sven, you see, has an answer for everything.'

'Hmm, I remember Sven,' Modeset started. 'Those were all the rage in Fogrise a few years back; they give you the same stupid answer each time. I think it's usually "I'm a happy bear" or something similar.'

'Not this one,' whispered the shopkeeper. 'Try it for yourselves if you don't believe me!'

Flicka looked the bear up and down.

'How does it work?' she asked.

'Simple! Ask it a question and then draw out the ring-pull. It will talk until the cord runs out.'

Flicka took the bear, ignoring Modeset's protests, and put her finger through the loop. Then she said, 'How much is that doggy in the window?' and let go.

The bear's voice was clear but strangely disquieting. It sounded like a death rattle, and spoke all in one narrowing breath.

'It's-a-toyshop-and-there-is-no-doggy-in-the-window-but-if-there-was-and-I'm-not-for-a-second-suggesting-that-there-is-then-it-would-probably-be-one-with-a-waggly-tail.'

'That's incredible!' said Flicka, hugging the bear and turning to the shopkeeper with a pleading grin. 'How much is it?'

'Fifty crowns . . .'

Modeset snatched the bear from Flicka's arms and drew out the cord.

'Why are you so damned expensive?' he enquired.

'You-pay-for-quality-in-this-life-so-don't-waste-my-time-pal-there-are-kids-out-there-who-need-answers.'

Modeset boggled at the toy and, incredulous, turned to the shopkeeper.

'Do you know what I think?' he said. 'I think these toys were perfectly ordinary to begin with and then you came along and made despicable alterations to them.'

The shopkeeper shook his head emphatically and reached for the bear, but Modeset lifted it beyond his grasp.

'I'll take these two,' he said. 'And I warn you, there'd better not be any more of them.'

He gave the bear and the dolly to Flicka, and had just finished paying for them when the door of the shop flew open and a number of heavily armed militiamen poured in.

Eleven

Viscount Curfew didn't smile very often. This fact would have come as no great surprise to the palace clerks; having seen the contessa they were amazed he managed it at all. Lady Curfew had an angular face that came complete with jutting jaw and a forehead which kept her feet dry. She also had watery eyes and thick lips, and something about her stance always gave people the impression of bad indigestion.

Thankfully, there were other amusements in the palace, and the chambermaids were always good for a giggle. In one morning Curfew had worked his way through kiss chase, hide-n-seek and a new method of hopscotch that involved leaping over dangerously large statues, putting his appetite for fun down to stress. It was an excuse with which everyone sympathized; just living in Dullitch did terrible things to people, only the gods knew what a nightmare it must be to run the place.

No, Curfew was a man determined to have fun; a pursuit enjoyed by none of his innumerable predecessors: wretches to a man, the last four in particular warranted scorn. First there had been Lord Morban, the hooded duke, a man so tortured by his own disfigurement that the only time the citizens ever saw his face was at his funeral. Bizarrely, there hadn't been a scratch on him. Lunatic. Next had come Baron Smother, a stout schizophrenic who despaired when he was given the throne and proceeded to attempt suicide in every one of the palace's forty-seven rooms, finally succeeding with a candlestick, in the study. Lunatic. Then along trundled Edwyn Vitkins, a retired soldier who declared war on Spittle and left to occupy the place before he'd even been sworn in! Thankfully for all concerned, he was dead in a fortnight. Last but not least, there was Modeset and the oft-fabled rat catastrophe. Ha! Three lunatics and a sadistic incompetent . . . some birthright. And the paintings!

Curfew peered up at the poorly finished portrait of Duke Vitkins. The Illmoor nobility approved of inter-breeding, partly because of social grace and partly because no one from the streets would have anything to do with them. This culminated in a royal family whose members all looked identical to one another and, consequently, only one portrait hung in the Dullitch throne room. It had seventy-three names underneath it.

Tiring of his surroundings, Curfew had turned to the papers. The news was grim: a statue he'd had erected outside the Candleford Boys' School had not been well received. Condemned by both the press and the public, some parents were claiming that their sons now walked the entire circumference of the city simply to avoid passing it on their way to school.

Curfew was just deciding whether or not to have a few editors hanged when Spires, administrator to the ducal throne, erupted into the chamber.

'I need to speak with you, Excellency,' he said. The tics, nervous twitches and various other facial distortions that plagued the man night and day were going into overdrive.

Curfew, who had scrunched the paper up so tight that his knuckles had paled, rounded on the little man like a dragon.

'DON'T YOU EVER KNOCK?' he bellowed.

'I'm sorry, Excellency,' said Spires, quickly. 'But this is important; your cousin Lord Modeset is here and he's requesting an audience.'

Curfew rolled his eyes.

'Why did we have to invite him back, exactly?'

'It's expected, Excellency. The duke is *family*, after all.'

'Ha! Yes, that's right. What else was it that you said to me? "He'll never accept it, Excellency. He wouldn't have the nerve to come back to Dullitch after the Rat

Catastrophe." Ha! Last time I listen to you! Tell him I'm busy.'

'We did, my lord, and he attacked the guards.'

'I beg your pardon?'

Spires fiddled nervously with his sleeves.

'We told him you were busy and he tried to force his way in, then he punched young Halvn and ran away, so we gave chase. Halvn caught up with him, but the duke's, er, *bodyguard*, gave the boy a damn good hiding.'

'Hmm . . . rough sort, is he?'

'*She*, Excellency.'

'Oh, for goodness' sa—'

'Exactly! Then they both ran away again. Fortunately, one of our boys saw them go into a toyshop on Royal Road, so we got a squad together and arrested them.'

'I see. Anything else?'

Spires nodded. 'We also found the duke's manservant. He was up a tree at the corner of Palace 'n' Royal, Excellency.'

Curfew put his head in his hands, and for a long time the secretary thought he'd fallen sleep. Eventually, one eye opened.

'Show him in.'

'And his staff, Excellency?'

'No, just Modeset. Lock the others up.'

'Yes, Excellency.' Spires reached the door and stopped, his fingers hovering inches from the brass handle. 'Should I, um, should I confiscate the items we found on him?'

'Hmm?'

'He was carrying a teddy bear and a small dolly, Excellency. When our men approached him, he brandished the latter as a weapon, claiming it could excrete acid. He was still fiddling with one of the legs when we managed to put the irons on him.'

'Very well; confiscate his toys and *then* show him in.'

'As you wish, Excellency.'

The secretary bowed low, and scurried from the room. Moments later, he returned with the duke in tow.

Twelve

Curfew paced back and forth before an immense circular window that commanded spectacular views of the cityscape, his lips twisted in a grim smile.

'Hmm . . . let us see what we have here: harassment of the palace guard, assault on an elf in the same occupation, two cases of evading the militia and one of threatening behaviour while brandishing a child's dolly. You have had a busy morning, Cousin.'

'Look,' said Modeset, struggling against the weight of his chains. 'If those imbeciles on the gate hadn't refused to admit me, none of the charges you just mentioned WOULD EXIST!'

'Hmm . . . yes. If I were you, Cousin, I'd take that tone of voice back to where it came from. I would remind you that you are now a guest here.'

'What? Oh yes, right. Apologies.' Modeset wasn't used to talking to anyone more important than himself; such people didn't exist within the boundaries of his own imagination.

'And, guesting,' Curfew continued, 'does require a certain amount of, how shall we say, host *tolerance*.'

'Ha! That's a joke! You haven't even paid my damn host!'

The viscount closed his eyes and clenched his fists tightly.

'An oversight on my part, I confess,' he said. 'The matter will be rectified in time. As for your behaviour . . .'

'I'll apologize to the guard I punched.'

'Yes, you will,' said Curfew, moodily. 'Also, you might think about keeping a low profile while you walk our busy streets. The people of Dullitch may have forgotten the rat catastrophe, but I'm sure your face will bring all those wonderful memories flooding back.' The viscount folded his arms and raised both eyebrows expectantly. 'I think you should leave now, Cousin,' he said.

Modeset flinched as Curfew snapped his fingers. Two imperial militiamen were suddenly all over him like a plague, throwing off chains and unscrewing manacles. Their task completed, Modeset found himself hoisted into the air and frogmarched through the echoing halls of the palace.

When he was back on firm ground, the elf guard came dawdling over to greet him.

'Well looky here,' he said. 'If it isn't his imperial lordship?'

Modeset straightened himself up.

The guard waited.

Modeset gritted his teeth.

The guard waited.

'Well?' he said eventually.

'What's that?' said the duke. 'If you think I'm apologizing to you, the rumours about elf intelligence must be spot on.'

The guard, although obviously angered, showed no sign of retaliation.

'That's OK,' it said. 'You can have your staff back the second you decide to change your mind.'

Before he could protest, Modeset was thrown out on to the seething streets of Dullitch, backwards.

Thirteen

Having wasted twenty crowns failing miserably to strike up a conversation with a young priestess on sabbatical, Jimmy Quickstint had retired to the smoky depths of the Rotting Ferret where he planned to drink himself towards slow oblivion while forging a halfway believable note of credit from the local spice merchant. With care and a generous amount of luck, he might even bluff himself a room for the night. The new landlord didn't look too sharp.

In some ways, Jimmy was glad to be rid of the job; digging graves'd never really suited him. Of course, it had been his first proper job (and would probably be his last), but these days it mainly served as a prop, something to fall back on when all else failed. Once upon a time, way back when, he'd been a thief, and even though he'd never really excelled, it was still the job he felt most proud of. He'd had some great times among the rooftop elite, and made some good friends along the way. Then, just after the terrible rat catastrophe, they'd kicked him out. O-U-T. Not so much as a by-your-leave.

Well, five years had passed since that fateful day. At first he'd adapted quite well, busking by day and telling stories at night. Now *that* was a profession, wandering from inn to inn, scratching a few crowns whilst propped against a fireplace with half a dozen drunks staring up at you, bleary-eyed. Then the market expanded, and suddenly people were fed up with hearing about the fiddler who trapped death in a sack or the baker's boy who beat the demons at poker. Children especially wanted violence, unprovoked and brutal, and if the elves didn't put the shoemaker through a third-floor window, they just weren't interested. Worse still, he'd actually found himself starting to adapt some of the old classics for this new blood-thirst. Snow White wasn't merely a pale princess, she was a Yowler assassin with vampiric tendencies, Little Red Riding Hood hadn't had any trouble with wolves since the day she acquired her grandmother's war-hammer, and – once they'd encountered Goldilocks – the three bears had absolutely no intention of ever going home again.

The whole profession had quickly developed into a battle between storytellers, who began to devise increasingly malevolent tales to entertain their audiences.

Jimmy'd got out just before the well ran dry. And here he was, a number of disastrous endeavours later.

Jobless.

He yawned and gazed down at the empty parchment he'd filched from the bar. As he suspected, the free quills handed out as samples by Counterfeit House weren't particularly good. He was just getting to grips with them, moving each one ghostlike over the crusty surface of the parchment, when his labours were interrupted.

'Mind if I join you?' said a familiar voice.

Jimmy looked up into the weathered face of Grab Dafisful, famed thief and Ferret regular during those murky hours between sunset and dawn. A lean man with a faint beard and extensive scarring, Grab was heavily rumoured to be one of the only thieves in the city worth forking out for.

'Don't s'pose I can stop you,' said Jimmy, miserably. 'But don't expect joviality.'

'I expect nothing from a fellow thief except sympathy and friendly conversation,' said Grab, pulling up a stool and peering at Jimmy's scrubby parchment with interest. 'I haven't seen you for an age! What're you up to these days?'

'Not much,' Jimmy snapped. 'And I'm a gravedigger; haven't been a thief since Granddad died.'

'It's quiet in here, tonight. How's your granddad?'

Jimmy looked up quickly and was about to give the thief a piece of his mind when he remembered Grab's bizarre tendency not to listen to anything unless he was being looked directly in the eye. It was a disconcerting habit, and one very good reason why the man didn't have any friends.

'Granddad's dead,' Jimmy reflected, uncomfortably staring the thief out. 'He went years ago, just after the whole rat episode. And I'm not a thief any more; now I dig holes for dead people.'

'Damn, I'm sorry.'

'About what? My granddad or the job?'

'Both.'

'Fine; sympathy accepted. Now, can I get on with writing this, please? Only, it doesn't seem to be possible for me to continue this conversation and do something else at the same time.'

'Eh? How d'you mean?'

'Never mind.'

Jimmy sighed and returned his attention to the parchment, while Grab ordered two flagons of ale.

At length, the silence was broken.

'Out with it, then,' Jimmy said, screwing up the parchment and tossing it across the floor. He leaned backwards, forcing his chair on to two legs. 'You never pay for a drink unless you're after something, so I might as well hear the pitch.'

Grab managed to look hurt for all of fifty seconds before his face cracked into a smile.

'All right,' he said. 'I need a favour. I've got myself into a bit of bother, as it happens.'

'There's a surprise.'

'No, I'm serious. Listen; last week I took on a job worth three hundred.'

'Crowns?' Jimmy's smile stayed exactly where it was, but the rest of his face sagged noticeably. 'How come I never got offered jobs like that when I was a thief?'

'Trust me,' Grab whispered conspiratorially. 'The risk matched the reward.'

'Oh?'

'Hell, yeah. I 'ad to go up to Grinswood.'

'What? That's at the other end of the continent!'

'Exac'ly. Then I 'ad to sneak through the deepest part of the forest and steal these baby lizards what can turn a man to stone if he isn't proper careful.'

Jimmy scratched his chin.

'Hmm . . . are you making this up?'

'No, I swear.'

'Well, even with all that danger, three hundred crowns is a pretty big fee. I mean, even after deductions there must be—'

'No deductions. Three hundred straight.'

Again, Jimmy's smile froze.

'The Rooftop Runners *always* pay a percentage to the Yowlers,' he said. 'After all, one's a part of the other.'

'Yeah, well, I know *that*, but this time it was different. This time I was workin' for the Yowlers themselves. It was hush-hush an' all. They came and got me in the night, took me to this church and told me what I had to do. Five of 'em, there were. Dead creepy an' all. I reckon most of the Yowlers don't even know 'bout it; I didn't see any o' the leaders there.'

Jimmy suddenly felt a deep chill in his spine.

'Are we getting to the bit where you need my help?' he asked, uneasily.

Grab nodded.

'So,' he continued. 'I'm in this forest, I've done the job and I'm on my way out. Then, just as I'm stopping for a gasp o' air, this bird lands on a tree branch.'

'Great gods,' Jimmy yawned. 'How much detail are we going into here?'

'Hang about; so this bird looks at me as if it knows what I done. Then off I go, outta the forest and I stops the night at this village inn 'bout three miles south o' the forest, an' there it is perched on the windowsill! The bird! And in the next village too! And now I'm back in Dullitch, and the damn thing's still out there! Hunting me down!'

'Is that it? A bird?' Jimmy asked, dumbfounded. 'Just ignore it.'

'I can't! What if it's waitin' to see where I'm takin' the sack? It might be a spy, workin' for the viscount or even the Yowler leaders!'

Jimmy shook his head. 'I don't think Viscount Curfew has many spies in the Grinswood.'

'Well, that's as maybe, but I don't want anything to go wrong with this job. If I make a mistake, lead an enemy to the door, so to speak, then bang goes my three hundred crowns. Now, if you was to—'

'Stop right there,' Jimmy interrupted. 'I think I can see where this is going and there's no way—'

'If we was to change clothes—'

'Not a chance.'

'And I unscrewed my mechanical arm—'

'No, I said, no.'

'Then you could put your head down and run for it. By the time the bird saw that you weren't me, I'd have delivered my sack an' I'd be two hundred and twenty-five crowns richer.'

Jimmy waited a moment while he worked this out.

'Let me get this straight: you're prepared to give me seventy-five crowns for impersonating you for an hour?'

'Yeah.'

'To get away from a bird.'

''S right.'

'You're insane. I'll do it.' He finished his ale and watched as Grab unscrewed his false limb. 'Where is this bird, anyway?'

'Up in the street.' Grab pointed towards the Ferret's staircase. 'It's perched on the sign over the Burrow Street Bakery, waitin' for me to come out. I'm convinced of it.'

'Yeah, yeah. We'll see. Can we at least find a quiet spot to change clothes? I don't fancy exhibiting my valuables in front of this crowd.'

Fourteen

Jimmy Quickstint was having a really bad night. Far from avoiding the barrowbird, his luck was such that he'd nearly walked straight into it. The situation called for all of his speed and cunning, so it was rather unfortunate that he didn't possess a great deal of either.

Then, to make matters worse, he'd dropped Grab's mechanical arm in Winding Way and had had to stoop to pick it up, all the while trying to keep his face groundward and maintain his friend's insane half-limp. It wasn't easy.

Finally, when he was at least six streets away from the Ferret and the crowds had begun to thicken, Jimmy spotted a convenient alleyway. Taking a deep breath and steeling all the muscles in his legs, he darted left, right, left, back, forwards, did a somersault and then nose-dived behind a pile of rubbish sacks just beyond the mouth of the alley. There, squatting in the shadows, he waited for the bird to fly past.

It didn't.

Time passed, and there was still no sign of the creature.

The Diamond Clock on Crest Hill struck eleven and, motionless, Jimmy waited.

Eventually, tiring of his awkward crouch, the gravedigger struggled to his feet and peered out into the street.

'Who're we lookin' for?' said a voice.

Jimmy turned and stared into the scruffy beak of the barrowbird. It had perched on a low wall opposite Jimmy's hiding place, and he was sure it was looking at him with malice.

'Game's up, genius,' it squawked. 'Worked like a treat; well done. Now stop soddin' about and tell me where your friend's gone.'

'Wh-what? What friend? I don't have any friends.'

'Don't mess with me, boy. You've no idea what you're getting involved in. I'm a magical bird, I am.'

'Oh.' Jimmy nodded. 'Then I expect you can find him yourself.'

There was an uncomfortable pause.

'I'll ask you once more, then I'll have your eyes out.'

Jimmy looked nervously about him, noticing on the edge of his vision that the gambling pits were opening for business.

'You don't look very fast,' he said to the bird, edging

carefully towards the alley mouth. 'I could probably outrun you.'

The bird hopped along the wall.

'Try it,' came the squawk.

'I might, at that,' Jimmy said, and darted off across the road. The bird took flight and flapped speedily after him. The chase had begun.

Jimmy ran like lightning.

The bird flew like a bullet.

Jimmy slipped through the door.

The bird hit it.

'Squawk! Squaark! I'll get you yet, sonny. However long it takes, I'll be waiting. You'll rue the day you ever pulled the wool over my beak!'

The barrowbird flapped itself against the wood a few times, then flew up to sulk on the swinging sign of a nearby tavern.

Just after three o'clock, two bouncers carried out the comatose figure of a young man, dumping it unceremoniously in the alley across the street. The taller of the pair was surprised to find that the young man'd acquired a mechanical arm in the process, which was especially confusing since their stow seemed to have all limbs intact.

Before they disappeared back inside the murky depths of their pit, one of the bouncers was sure that he heard a menacing and somehow *feathery* cackle.

Fifteen

Karuim's Church was unique in that it was the only building on Oval Square to have its entrance in Bark Street. Well, unique was perhaps too strong a word. After all, the buildings that occupied the other side of the square would've been hard pressed to have their entrances on Bark Street without some sort of magic door in use. Nevertheless, Karuim's spurned the palace which dominated Oval Square, and many took this to be indicative of the Yowlers' notorious defiance in the face of royalty. Not that the church was wholly Yowler-run: it hadn't been so since a breakaway faction had claimed it little more than a year since.

The church itself was an eyesore, black as pitch and thoroughly shapeless, with an ugly gaping hole where its doors should have been. Worshippers walked into this cave mouth and through the ensuing tunnel system before emerging into the dark expanse of the sanctuary proper.

It was a frightening journey, especially for Grab Dafisful, who was increasingly of the opinion that his every move was being watched, and not by a bird. In fact, he couldn't help but feel, as he was about to deliver his sack to the church's vestry, that the kind of eyes currently monitoring his progress were the sort that travelled back and forth to a belt dagger between glimpses. Sweat beading on his forehead, Grab reached for his own blade.

'Hmm . . . I'd move that hand back pretty sharpish if I were you, especially since you've only got the one.'

Grab froze; the voice had come from behind him. His hand hovered an inch or so above his belt.

'Throw down the knife,' the voice commanded. 'You shouldn't bring such things into a house of the gods.'

The dagger clanked on to the stone floor, followed by three smaller blades and a set of knuckledusters.

'Well, well, well,' the voice continued. 'You do come prepared, Mr Dafisful. Now, please deposit your burden in the pew to your extreme left. Very good. Now, face front and prepare to answer a few questions.'

While Grab did as he was told, a hand snaked around from behind him and snatched up the sack.

'Where's my money?' he shouted, being careful not to move a muscle.

'All in good time,' said the voice. 'First, the questions.'

There followed some sort of commotion in the

shadows, before Grab noticed two cloaked shapes moving up the aisles on either side of him. Once in the centre of the sanctuary, they separated, to stand not more than six feet apart. When given occasion to speak, they spoke together, more, Grab fancied, to disguise their individual voices than to create an air of mystery. It worked; the only thing he could be sure of was that one was male, the other female.

'Thief Dafisful. You have done as the brotherhood commanded?'

Grab nodded.

'I have.'

'You have retrieved no less than ten Batchtiki from the Grinswood?'

'I have.'

'You were not followed?'

'What? Er . . . not exactly, no.'

A male voice this time, solo. 'What do you mean by "not exactly"? Either you were followed, or you were not.'

Grab's movements became very fidgety.

'There *was* this bird, you see, and—'

'A bird?'

'Yeah, and I thought it was—'

'As in "flap flap" bird?'

'Er . . . yes.'

The female voice took up the questioning. 'We have no interest in birds. When we asked if you were followed, we were talking bipeds.'

Grab's features creased like a brown paper bag.

'No, I'm sure I wasn't followed by any of them.'

'Good. And you spoke of your endeavours to no one?'

'Nope. Definitely not. No, siree. I'm not stupid, me. I spoke to no one. Well, no one worth speaking of?'

'So, in fact, you *did* tell somebody.'

'Um . . . sort of. Yeah.'

There was a collective sigh.

'More than one person?'

'No. Just the one, I swear. Just Jimmy, he's a friend of mine, ex-thief, understands perfectly. He won't tell a soul.'

'Hmm . . . we shall see. For now, you may go.'

'Hey! What about my money?'

'You will find it beside the decorative font on your way out.'

Grab nodded and turned to leave, muttering to himself about conspiracies and the kind of people who lurked in shadows. He didn't see a soul on his way out of the church but, even as he collected his money, he felt they were watching him. In the shadows.

As soon as Grab had left the sanctuary, two dark hoods were drawn back in unison.

'Your thief talks too much,' said the female voice. 'He'll have to be silenced.'

'And his friend?' echoed her male counterpart. 'This Jimmy? A danger, you think?'

'Undoubtedly.'

'We can't just leave it and hope. We're too near!'

'Exactly.'

'Two jobs for Mixer, then?'

'Ha! If our little gnome's as good as you say he is, Lopsalm, I'm sure he's dealing with it already...'

'Oh, he is, my dear. I can assure you of that.'

'He'll need to be fast, mind; thieves like Grab can be wily and resourceful.'

Lopsalm turned in the darkness.

'A good job we dispatched Moors and Edwy, then, isn't it?'

Sixteen

Grab had a terrible feeling in the pit of his stomach. Keeping a tight grip on the money pouch with his remaining hand, he began to run.

Footsteps echoed behind him.

On he ran, urging his tired body through the pain barrier.

The footsteps increased with him, and he heard the distinctive sound of a crossbow being primed.

Grab peered over his shoulder, caught the merest glimpse of a small figure as it nipped into a doorway. Then he started to run, very fast.

The streets, slippery and lashed with rain, were deserted; they flittered past as Grab hurtled around corners and leaped over bins in a frantic dash for the safety of the market square. He knew the stalls would be

long gone, but there were *always* people in the square.
There *had* to be.

Incredibly, the rainstorm picked up. Grab thought he
saw a shape up ahead; large, almost impossibly so. Was it
a troll or a person? Difficult to tell. Grab strained to see
through the veil of rain. Yes, a person. Definitely. Thank
the gods. Now, if he could just put on another burst of
speed . . .

The shape lumbered forward, and Grab almost fell
into it.

'Hey, watch it.'

'I'm sorry,' Grab managed, righting himself and
standing back to stare in awe at the size of the human
mass before him. 'There's someone after me . . .'

'I can't see anybody.'

Grab swung round and squinted into the rain.

'No, well. I could swear I was being followed.' He
turned back. 'Anyway, it's a nice nigh—'

The lumbering shape threw out a fist so hard that
Grab almost achieved flight as he flew backwards,
landing in the middle of a collection of rubbish bins with
a resounding crash.

The rain hammered down. As Grab fought to get to
his feet, he noticed that his noisy collision with the
rubbish had failed to attract even the merest hint of
attention; not a light in a window, not the creak of a
door. Grab moaned as he regained his footing.

Shapes loomed up ahead; the large man who'd hit him

had now been joined by a second, slimmer figure. Grab turned on his heels and started to run, hopelessly, back towards the temple. After a few steps, he hesitated, then stopped and peered over his shoulder. The two men weren't moving; they were simply standing there, closing off the end of the street.

Grab tried to think clearly, his head still fuzzy from the strength of the big man's punch. They were obviously herding him towards a greater danger. He shook his head, then turned back and practically walked into the gnome.

Mixer was standing in the street ahead, his brass teeth glinting in the glow of the street lamp beside him. He was holding a large and very nasty-looking crossbow.

Grab turned, yet again, and ran. His hope was to break through the human barricade up ahead. He made a last, desperate dash.

Lightning split the sky, and thunder echoed through the clouds. The rain came down hard . . .

. . . and so did Grab Dafisful.

'Ahhhh!'

The bolt struck home, spearing into the thief's back and forcing him forward. Grab gasped, his legs folded under him. Rain plastering his hair to his forehead, he laid a hand flat against the cobbles and tried to push himself up, but the gnome was on him.

Thunder boomed overhead, announcing its warning to any citizens who hadn't already turned their mirrors to face the wall.

'Ahhh! No! Mercy, I beg you!'

Mixer drove a boot into the small of the thief's back, reloaded the crossbow and aimed it at his head. Then he pulled the trigger.

There was a sickening thud.

As the last of the rain came down, the corpse of Grab Dafisful was dragged into a nearby doorway and left propped up against the door like a stuffed dummy. Mixer smiled at his handiwork, and promptly departed.

Part Two

The Duke and the Detective

One

Modeset was fuming, and with good reason.

He'd been walking through the streets all night. He was dirty, hungry and, worst of all, he didn't have anyone else to blame. All he had were choices. He didn't want to go back to the Steeplejack Inn without the others (the Innkeeper was enough of a pain as it was) and he certainly had no intention of loitering anywhere near the palace, so he'd decided to kick off his new day with a depressed stroll around the harbour district instead.

It wasn't a bad day, by Dullitch standards, and the sun glinted off the highly polished paintwork of the *Mostark*, the viscount's supreme galleon. Modeset wondered if he'd ever own such a ship again. Considering his current finances, a rowing boat seemed the more likely option, if they hired them out.

Heading along the quay, he came upon a small platform where two dwarfs were unloading a heavy crate of Legrash Ale. They tried to lift the crate, failed and then proceeded to drag it off the platform, accompanied by an orchestra of grunts and groans. Modeset asked if he could lend a hand, expecting them to decline.

'You're on,' said the older of the two, a dwarf with a beard almost down to his ankles. 'Get at the side and guide us in.'

Reluctantly, Modeset did as he was told. The dwarfs took a breath, lifted again and set off, remarking on how the ale seemed even heavier than before. They were right, too; Modeset didn't like to admit it, but after the first few feet they were actually carrying him as well. Some of these dockers, he reflected, had more sinews than sense.

At length, the crate was set down and the dwarf with the beard consulted a tattered scroll fastened to the lid.

'I'm done believin' it,' he said. 'What kind of grizzled nut am I?'

His colleague waited for the bad news.

Modeset, sensing the possibility of further involvement, had already taken a step back.

'This is supposed to go on to Spittle,' the first dwarf said.

'So?' said the other docker, moodily.

'So, it's the Day of Storms, right? Day of Storms cargo for Spittle. See any connection there? We should be in

Warehouse Five, not Warehouse Six. Let's move it out. C'mon.'

The second dwarf prepared to lift the crate, then stopped and looked about him.

'Where's the bloke who was helpin' us?' he said.

'Dunno,' said the first. 'Maybe he fell under the crate.'

They burst into a roaring, gut-rooted laughter and, after four attempts, carried the crate over to Warehouse Five.

Meanwhile, Modeset hunkered down in the shadows. Either through fate or fortune, he'd found himself in the warehouse that the scroll had mentioned. What harm could it do to take a look around?

Apart from an ageing hill troll unpacking barrels in the north-west corner, the warehouse was deserted. Crates of various shapes and sizes, piled haphazardly with barely an inch between stacks, reached almost to the rafters in every direction. The trick, he decided, was to know where to start in such a maze of merchandise.

Stay away from Warehouse Six. The words rang in his ears, but they offered no clue. Still, he suspected he'd recognize something to stay well away from as soon as he got on top of it.

Time passed.

Modeset squeezed between row upon row of crates, studying the little scrolls attached to each one. As it turned out, the cargo came from all over Illmoor and included unmarked stock from Legrash, Spittle, the

Gleaming Mountains, the Twelve, Shadewell, Carafat, Grinswood and Sporring.

Time passed.

Modeset stalked the aisles. It was beginning to dawn on him that there was a lot more to this investigating lark than met the eye, when a voice interrupted his train of thought.

''Scuse me,' it said. 'This is private prop'ty and you're a trusspisser.'

Modeset had his answer all worked out.

Unfortunately, when he turned around to supply it, the troll head-butted him.

As red mist drifted over Modeset's field of vision, his hulking attacker stomped off to look for a crate winch.

Two

Elsewhere, morning found Mixer in a quiet corner of Mudsen Mill, the city's premier café. When the stout (but not unpleasant-looking) waitress had delivered two squares of charred toast, he peered around for any obvious signs of attention before producing a tattered notebook from the recesses of his jerkin.

Flipping open the top leaf, he ran a grubby finger down the hastily scribbled list of names. Then, plucking a tiny length of lead from behind his ear, he put a neat line through the last two.

That was the inventor *and* the thief out of the way. Now there were only a few loose ends to worry about.

He studied the remaining list and considered his options. As far as he could see, there was one 'urgent' and a possible 'pending'.

The loftwing wouldn't wait much longer; in fact, Mixer had already decided that the next time he was followed, the investigator would get what was coming to him; indubitably. Then there was the boy: Dafisful *had* spent a long time talking to the young wastrel in the saloon bar of the Ferret. He might have told him anything; hell, he might have told him *everything*. So: another one to add to the list. If only there was a little more time! Still, needs must . . .

First things first, he told himself. Breakfast – the most important meal of the day.

Mixer took one last glance at the notebook before returning it to his jerkin pocket. Then he ordered a coffee to go with his charcoal.

Three

Jimmy Quickstint, half barefoot on the cold cobbles of
the alley in which he'd spent the night, was livid. Of
course, he'd enjoyed himself at first. Everybody did. This
was because, for sheer incredible logic, gambling was
hard to beat. You came in off the street with naff all
except three acorns and a foot infection, and in less than
fifteen minutes you had a bag of gold, six illegitimate
children and a couple of empty cottages in lower Dullitch
with rental possibilities. That, of course, was if you were
endowed with luck, knew how to play and carried enough
loaded dice to take out a small jetty.

Jimmy wasn't, didn't and hadn't. He'd been carried
from the Pits of Primo Don barely three hours after
he went in, having parted with two shoes, one sock
and his left eyebrow. The last, he'd been assured, he

could claim back at a later date, in exchange for the seventeen crowns he owed Logoff the Merchant. Additionally, to form a nice creamy topping on his elephantine disaster of a day, he now found himself hungry and alone in a part of the city he had hitherto only seen on the second-hand maps outside the Cartography School.

He was about to make a move, pretty sharpish, when a frighteningly familiar voice said: 'You're up, then?'

Jimmy turned slowly on his heels and found himself staring into the beak of the barrowbird.

'Leave me ALONE!'

'Shan't.'

'Damn you!'

'Nice.'

'No, I mean it! Damn you to hell.'

'Colourful; do you blaspheme professionally or are you still on the amateur circuit?'

Jimmy extended a finger to support his annoyance. 'Stuff this in your beak and curse you, you emaciated feathered twit.'

'Listen, you can damn me all you like. I told you last night that I wouldn't be easy to shake off.'

'Yes, but what do you want?'

'Your friend with the limp.'

'But I don't know where he is!'

'Then find him, and I'd be pretty sharpish if I were you. I'm not a patient bird.'

Jimmy fell against the alley wall and allowed himself to slide down it.

'This is ridiculous!' he gasped. 'Do you have any idea how big Dullitch is? He could be anywhere!'

'He's *your* friend. You must know where he hangs out.'

Jimmy shook his head.

'Thieves aren't like that,' he said. 'They only come to you when they need something, and I've already done Grab a favour, remember?'

The barrowbird flapped a bit, then appeared to reach a decision.

'You'll have to go back to the tavern,' it squawked.

Jimmy shrugged. 'It's a long shot.'

'Do you know any short ones?'

'No.'

'Then get movin'!'

Four

Viscount Curfew sighed deeply.

'I take it you have some bad news, Spires?' he said.

His royal secretary paused in the doorway, unsure of whether he should risk an entrance.

'Wh-why do you say that, Lord?'

'You only come to see me on such occasions.'

'Oh, I . . .'

Curfew raised an eyebrow. 'Well? Do go on.'

'Um, right, er, the fact is, that, in fact, the point being . . .'

'Quickly, please. Before one of us dies.'

'Yes, Sir. Of course. What would you like first? The atrocious end of the news or its abysmal beginnings?'

'Start with the atrocious and work your way backwards.

That way you have at least a thirty per cent chance of survival.'

Spires closed the door to the chamber behind him and took a seat on the base of a marble plinth, clearing his throat in the process.

'A short while ago I fired one of the scribes, a young lady by the name of Lauris.'

'On what grounds?'

'Um . . . the palace grounds, Sir.'

'No, you idiot, *what grounds did you have to fire her*?'

'Oh right, I see. Well, our people were watching her for some time, and I knew, second hand, of at least three activities that she could have been fired for, but I actually *caught* her signing import orders.'

'*Import orders?* For what?'

Spires scratched nervously at his arm.

'Machinery, sir. Tin, iron, some enchanted bronze too, if I recall; all sorts of nonsense. Unfortunately she burnt the paperwork shortly before we confronted her, and now we can't find out where she stored these . . . *supplies*. Wherever it was, they've probably been moved on by now.'

'And the girl?'

'She disappeared, Sir. The spies observed that several palace-stamped scrolls disappeared at around the same time.'

'Why on earth wasn't she fired before?'

'Well, the fact is, Excellency, she did a lot of very positive things for us.'

'Such as?'

'Well, um, trade deals and the like. In fact, it was Lauris who found out about your new statue and suggested that we had it moved down from Spittle to put in the ci— Why are you looking at me like that, Excellency?'

'Never mind. It just seems curious then that she made such a nuisance of herself. It doesn't really add up, does it?'

'No, Excellency. Not at all.'

'And now she's probably up to something dodgy with our stamped scrolls, no doubt. What use would they be?'

The servant took a deep breath.

'No use whatsoever *inside the city*, Excellency. As for foreign powers, well, I expect she could send a few bogus war declarations, but nothing any of the major cities would take seriously without a herald to back it up.'

'So no threat there, then. How long since she vacated the palace?'

Spires fidgeted nervously on the little platform.

'Approximately two weeks, give or take a day,' he said.

Curfew shut his eyes for a moment, then opened them again. 'And you only thought to tell me about it now?'

'Um, I didn't want to alarm you, Excellency.'

'Is that right? I'm assuming you've taken steps to find this girl?'

'Of course, Excellency. We hired an investigator to track her down; we thought it might be better to work quietly so as not to attract undue attention.'

'Has he turned up anything?'

'Yes and no, Excellency, yes and no. He called at her house on North Street, aiming to search for some clue as to her whereabouts, but when he arrived he found a gnome torching the place.'

Curfew's expression twisted into the half smirk of the intrigued.

'A gnome.'

'Yes, Excellency, a gnome.'

'And did he capture this gnome?'

'No, the report says that he made no attempt to do so. He suspected that if he followed this *gnome*, then maybe it would lead him to Lauris herself.'

'Hmm . . . a fair conclusion, I suppose. Is that all?'

'No, milord. The whole thing has become quite a bit more complicated. Mr Obegarde, that's the investigator, he's been asking questions up at City Hall, and they say that this gnome is the caretaker at Karuim's.'

Curfew's expression suddenly froze.

'That's a Yowler building, isn't it?'

'Yes, Excellency, which is why I thought it best to tell you about all this in the first place. We might have a real problem, here.'

'I see.' The viscount rose from his chair and, marching over to the window, stared out at the steeples of the great church. 'This girl, this . . . Lauris. You must talk to everyone in the palace who worked with her, Spires,' he said. 'Friends, enemies, rivals, I don't care who they are,

I want a complete report on her movements. We need to know if she has or had any connection with the Yowler Brotherhood. Leave no stone unturned!'

The secretary bowed low and hurriedly vacated the chamber, leaving the viscount to his thoughts.

Five

Modeset awoke to find himself in a crate. His eyes ached, and drums beat a steady rhythm inside his head. He moaned, brought a hand to his chin and wiped away a crusted mixture of blood and spittle.

I'm a duke, he thought. I'm royalty! They can't get away with treating me like this! I'm off to the palace, and Curfew will HAVE to listen this time because I'm family and because I'm of the blood! Someone's going to have to pay; someone like that elf, someone who, someone . . . SOMEONE GET ME OUT OF THIS STINKING CRATE.

He aimed both feet at the lid and kicked frantically, elbowing the sides for good measure. Just when he was beginning to make some headway, he heard the faintest hint of a whisper. At first, he thought it might be the wind, but then, ever so slightly, the volume increased.

'Stpt.'

Modeset strained to listen.

'opit—'

'What? Is someone out there?'

The next time the voice spoke, it was clearly audible.

'Stop it,' it said. 'Stop wriggling. Don't move another inch.'

'What do you mean "Don't move another inch"?' screamed Modeset. 'Help! Get me out of here!'

'Quieten down!' said the voice, increasing in urgency. 'The dockers are patrolling tonight and I can't handle all of 'em. Stay quiet and they'll pass.'

'Tonight? You mean I've been out all day? Damn that troll!'

'Shh! Listen, you don't know where you are.'

Modeset fidgeted inside his prison.

'Don't be ridiculous,' he said. 'I'm in a crate.'

'OK,' the voice continued. 'Let's put it another way. You don't know where the crate is.'

There followed a few seconds of expectant silence.

'Why?' asked Modeset, voice quavering. 'Where is it?'

'Roughly? About twenty-five feet off the ground. So stay still.'

A brief scuffling ensued and Modeset suspected that he heard a rope being winched. There was a sharp creak and suddenly he felt the crate move in the air. After a time, it swung left, leaving him with an empty feeling in the pit of his stomach. Then, slowly at first, it began to descend.

'OK,' said the voice. 'Let's get this off.'

The head of a crowbar bit into the wood and the lid of the crate was wrenched clear. Modeset pulled himself up and looked out at a dark shadow. His eyes travelled from shiny black boots to a thatch of jet black hair that crowned the shadow in all its menacing glory. Recognition dawned very gradually.

'It's you! Why are you dressed like that?'

The loftwing looked down at himself.

'I always dress like this,' he said. 'It's part and parcel of the job. If I don't dress like this, people won't recognize me. Now, may we dispense with the pleasantries?'

Modeset frowned, and nodded, before a fist like bunched steel sent him careering back into the crate.

Obegarde stepped forward and pulled the duke up again.

'I thought I told you to keep your nose out of this,' he snapped, supporting Modeset by the base of his chin. 'What is it with dukes? I've known a few, and you're all the same. You go gallivanting around on the merest whim, sticking your noses into every kind of trouble, as if the world owes you a favour. Well, if I remember rightly, Dullitch certainly doesn't owe you any favours.'

Modeset wriggled free and shook his head.

'It's not what you think,' he said, still in shock and

spitting blood with every second word. 'I got here by accident.'

'A likely story.'

'No, it's true. This afternoon, after I got arrested—'

'You?' Obegarde's half smile came as a definite relief. 'How did you get arrested? Parked your carriage over a trade route or something?'

'I punched a guard,' Modeset managed.

'Really? I'm impressed, but that still doesn't explain what you're doing here . . .'

'Yes, well—'

'And you've only got five minutes until I lose my famous kind streak.'

The duke tried to explain.

Obegarde pretended to listen.

'Well,' he said when Modeset had brought his tale up to date. 'Now you're here, you might as well see what it is our friend doesn't want me to find.'

He took a step back and gestured behind him.

Modeset squinted into the darkness and shrugged.

'I don't see anything,' he said.

'You sure?'

'Of course I'm sure! There's nothing there! I know because that's the way I came in. If there was a crate standing on its own, I'd have seen it.'

Obegarde's grin stayed right where it was.

'It's not a crate,' he said. 'Look again.'

Modeset stared hard at the wall of the warehouse,

except that it wasn't the wall of the warehouse. It was the back of something. Something huge.

'Ye gods!' he cried. 'What is it? It's enormous.'

'You're telling me,' said Obegarde, scratching his granite forehead.

'I must have walked right past it!'

'So did I, three times. For some reason, you just can't comprehend it at first.'

'But what in the name of the gods is it?'

The loftwing shrugged.

'A machine of some kind,' he said. 'It's camouflaged to melt in with the warehouse wall. Harbour Master's an elf, so there's no way he doesn't know about it ... which leads me to believe that the owner of this monster holds sway over at least one high-ranking member of the Mariners' Consortium.'

'It's glowing,' remarked Modeset, taking a step back.

'Yeah, it does seem to do that, on and off,' said Obegarde. 'At a guess, I'd say it's part magic and part machine. There's a lens on the top, a lever on the side and tubes all over the place. It's got me puzzled, I don't mind admitting.'

Modeset narrowed his eyes.

'I don't like the look of it,' he said. 'There's something instinctively destructive in the shape. Who do you think owns it? Your rock-thrower?'

'Could be, could be,' said Obegarde, nodding. 'He visits it every night. That's what first led me here. And he always brings a book. Does nothing with it, mind. It's almost as if he just brings the thing so he doesn't have to leave it at home.'

Modeset nodded. 'Odd. Well, um, how am I going to get out of here exactly?'

The investigator grinned.

'You're not,' he said. 'You're gonna keep watch while I break into the Harbour Master's office. I need to see if there's any record of this monstrosity in the holding log.'

The first kick wrenched the cottage door from its hinges, the second sent it crashing to the floor.

'I thought you said the dockers were watching this place,' Modeset whispered.

'They are,' said Obegarde, with a shrug. 'That's why I knew we wouldn't have any trouble getting in.'

'I'm sorry I—'

'Dockers aren't generally too bright. They're big and slabby, but not too quick on the brain trigger.'

The Dullitch Harbour Master's office was a bit of a dump; Modeset couldn't see for anchors.

'Here we are,' called Obegarde, clambering over the desk to study the heavy logbook. 'Hmm, recent entries . . . Aha!'

Modeset kept watch, peering around the fractured door like a nervous whippet.

'Interesting,' said the investigator, scratching his concrete chin.

'What? What is it?'

'Well, you need two signatures to legally deposit a crate, especially when it's unlikely to leave the city. The machine is logged in as Herman's Stare. There's a brief disclosure note signed by one Augustus Vrunak, address in upper Dullitch. The other signature's too blurred to make out, but the address is definitely Karuim's.'

'The church next to the palace?' Modeset asked.

'Hmm . . . my last stop, I think. Night's almost over.' He looked up and saw Modeset backing out of the door. 'Hey! Where're you going?'

'Home!' said the duke. 'And it's no use you trying to stop me; I'm tired and I want to get some sleep.'

Obegarde rolled his eyes.

'You're joking, right?' he said. 'Besides, I need some help here; you might as well just come with me. We'll both head back to the Steeplejack when we're done.'

'No!' Modeset shook his head. 'I'm off *now*. None of this has anything to do with me. *You* can go wherever you like.'

'OK, OK,' said the investigator. 'But you *are* involved now, whether you like it or not, so can you at least do me a favour?'

The duke sighed.

'That depends; what kind of favour? Does it involve me dressing up, spending time in a confined space or becoming embroiled in a street fight?'

'No.' Obegarde shook his head and passed him a small

square of paper torn from the logbook. 'Check out this Vrunak fellow for me.'

'What, now?'

'Not necessarily. Get your precious sleep; you can go tomorrow morning. Here's the address.'

Modeset was about to decline, but when he saw the look on the loftwing's rugged face, he thought better of it.

Six

The Rotting Ferret was bustling with activity. Chas Firebrand's decision to sell the subterranean inn to a family of goblins from Phlegm had seemed disastrous on paper, but Frowd Fjin was certainly a greenskin with talent. In a little over five years, he'd turned the place from an oft-avoided fighting pit into a respected nightclub, complete with orc bouncers, elf waitresses and even a troglodyte cabaret group.

Jimmy was miserable; he'd been waiting at the inn for hours and there was not even the merest hint of a sign of Grab Dafisful. Worse still, he knew that the barrowbird was waiting outside and no matter how many ingenious ways he invented of leaving the Ferret, his feathered curse would eventually catch up with him.

'So let me get this straight,' he muttered to the gnome

who'd taken a seat beside him and promptly ordered a round. 'You're saying that you can smash the green bottle above the bar, third along on the right, without anyone knowing it was you? Get out.'

Mixer waved him into silence.

'A crown says I can, a drink says I can't.'

'Done.'

The gnome quickly produced a light but intricate-looking crossbow, then lowered his head and fired off a shot, thrusting the weapon under the table before the merest hint of breaking glass.

'OI!' bellowed the landlord, a swarthy half-ogre. 'WHO DID THAT? WE'LL HAVE NO SUCH SPORT IN 'ERE!'

Jimmy turned, mouth still agape, to stare at the gnome.

'Drinks're on me, then,' he said. 'Incredible. Just incredible.'

Mixer shrugged.

'You think that's impressive,' he started, drawing closer to the gravedigger and lowering his voice to a conspiratorial whisper. 'I can make the bells of Karuim's toll without even touching them.'

'Rubbish; now that *is* impossible.'

'Ha! That's what Grab said this morning. He's laughing on the other side of his face now!'

'Grab? Not Grab Dafisful, the thief?'

'Yeah, the very same. Why, d'you know him?'

'Know him? He ... er ... he owes me seventy-five crowns!'

Mixer's tiny eyes lit up.

'Oh, it's you he owes!' The gnome tapped at his shiny brass teeth. 'He said as much; just between us, he's hiding up on the roof of Karuim's Church. I met him this morning when I was doing some routine maintenance work for the council. In fact, I'm due back there in a minute. D'you fancy joining me? You can have a word with Grab and then we can see who takes this incredibly fine piece of weaponry home. What d'you say?'

Jimmy, ever the sucker for a gamble, took the proffered weapon in his hands, and looked it over. It was made of Chakiwood, the poisoned bark of the Red Lime Tree. Rare; expensive. It had to be worth at least a hundred crowns.

'You're on,' Jimmy agreed, passing the crossbow back to the gnome with a nod.

'We'll call it a deal, then,' said Mixer, staring dispassionately at the barmaid as she delivered their long-awaited tankards of ale. 'Unless you want to start small; I can't imagine a fellow like you has too much gold.'

Jimmy tried to keep a straight face, which was difficult with a mug like his. One thing everyone in the city knew about Jimmy, apart from the fact that he used to be a thief and was reasonably good with a shovel, was his marked annoyance at anyone suggesting that he was penniless.

He raised one eyebrow and tried to focus on the Rotting Ferret's rowdy clientele.

'I'm doing OK, as a matter of fact,' he lied. 'So let's talk turkey; when do you want me to witness your terrible failure at the church? Now?'

A silence settled over the table.

'Well, there's no time like the present. Isn't that what they say?'

'Sure, OK. Give me a minute to pay the piper; I'll be right back.'

'Result,' Mixer said, with an evil grin. 'Hurry up though, I can't hang around all night.'

Jimmy nodded, jumped out of his chair and dashed through the bar. Once safely beyond the grimy door which led to the Ferret's condemned latrines, he hurtled along a dank passage, up three flights of half crumbled steps, past a dingy back door, over the wall in the Ferret's beer garden, down the alley which clung to its western side and out into the street that contained the inn's decrepit entrance doors.

The barrowbird spotted him immediately, alighting from its perch on a first-floor windowsill of a bakery across the road.

'Anything?' it squawked. 'I haven't seen him go in.'

'He's not there,' Jimmy hurriedly confided. 'But I'm talking to a gnome who's gonna take me to him.'

'A gnome?'

'Yeah.'

'What, just like that?'

'Yes!'

'No questions asked?'

'Yes, I mean, *NO*!'

'Does the gnome know anything about the group that hired him?'

'I don't KNOW!'

'Can't you find out?'

'NO!'

'Why not?'

'Look, it's simple. He thinks he owes me money!'

'Who, the gnome?'

'Grab, damn it! Why don't you listen?'

'I am listening; why can't you speak properly?'

'Don't start with me! I'm doing you a favour here.'

'Ha! You dug your own grave, boy. Now *you* listen. Why don't you follow this dwarf—'

'It's a gnome, and I'm GOING TO!!!!!'

'Right, and then I'll follow the pair of you.'

'D'you think so? Gad, and I thought I was sharp. Can I go now?'

'No, wait! Just hang on a minute; how did you get out?'

'I lied; told him I was going to the latrine.'

'Right. So hadn't you better get back inside then, so we can follow him when he leaves?'

'Yes! That's what I'm saying!'

'Well, don't let me keep you.'

Jimmy rolled his eyes. Then he raced back down the alley, leapt the wall, shouldered past the door, fell down the stairs, hurtled along the corridor, bumped his way through the bar, landed on the three-legged stool opposite the gnome, and promptly fell off it.

Mixer swallowed a gulp of ale.

'That was quick,' he said.

$\mathcal{S}e\mathcal{N}en$

Night yawned . . .

When Modeset returned to the Steeplejack Inn, he found Flicka waiting for him.

The duke had always had a curious relationship with the girl, partly because he found her very beautiful, but mostly because he didn't feel at all comfortable with young women. Any women, come to that.

However, observing her now as she stood in the entrance hall of the inn with her hair plastered to her face and her ragged clothes heavy with rain, Modeset was beginning to understand what all the fuss was about. The girl was healthy, that much was certain.

'Well, I say, what a surprise,' he began. 'I was very, very worried about you, Flicka. In fact, I was just this minute coming to get you out of the dungeons and, whoosh-adacadava, here you are. Most impressive.'

Flicka raised a thick eyebrow. Her brown eyes glistened.

'On your way to getting us out?' she said. 'How thoughtful, my lord. Odd, though, I seem to recall the palace being in the opposite direction.'

Modeset nodded quickly.

'Yes, well of course, it *is*,' he said. 'But I was planning to get some shut-eye first, you know, conserve a bit of energy.'

'That's fine,' said Flicka, beaming. 'I'll grab the carriage from the stables and you can get some rest on the way to the guardhouse.'

'The guardhouse?'

'Yes. They've still got Pegrand, and they won't let him out until you apologize to the guard. They only let me out because I'm a woman.'

She swept back her hair with both hands, bunched up two fistfuls of it and secured the resulting locks with a length of twine. Then, still grinning, she took a step towards the door.

Modeset held up a hand.

'We're not going to the palace,' he said. His tone was set in lead.

'What? But you said you were—'

'It's not done for a duke to apologize and, besides, that guard had it coming. All elves are deviants.'

'That's a rotten attitude for a duke, especially here. It's not right to persecute any of Nature's children.'

'Not right? You can't rely on Nature, you know. Just look at what she did to Pegrand. Besides, we don't have time for this nonsense or to mess about rescuing people. I need some sleep and so do you.'

Flicka looked suddenly wretched.

'What about Pegrand?' she said.

'I'll get him out in the morning,' said Modeset, after a pause.

'You promise?'

'Yes. Now go!'

He watched her turn and make for the stairs, listening for any hint of a giggle. He was about to retire himself when the Innkeeper came barrelling out of the dining hall.

'Cursed nuisance,' he spat. 'Shutters broken, puts me out, 'nother hole in my purse. The sheer cheek of it . . .'

'Yes,' said the duke. 'I'm terribly sorry if that puts you out.'

'Puts me out, you say? Puts me out? You're a damn nuisance.'

'Yes, again, my apologies. Any chance of a new room tonight?'

'Any chance? No chance. Sleep in the alley, far as I'm concerned. You're a damn curse, the lot o' you.'

Modeset shot forward. The movement was sudden and unexpected, and the Innkeeper found himself pinned against the hall wall.

'Now listen up,' snapped the duke. 'I've told you you'll

see your money, so get this straight: you'll give me a new room, a better room with a nice soft bed and a proper window, you'll stop moaning, you'll be pleasant to my staff and, if I get even the slightest hint that you've been spitting in the wine, they'll find you where I leave you. Now, do we have an understanding?'

The Innkeeper swallowed and Modeset thought he could just make out a nod.

Eight

Dullitch was a city full of filth and, as Obegarde could testify, it all floated to the surface at downtime.

Downtime. He repeated the word over and over, working it into a steady rhythm. His boots threw up splashes of water as they hit the puddle-strewn cobbles.

Downtime was the affectionately named period between midnight and sunup when some of Dullitch's darkest, weirdest and most nocturnally bound citizens began to stir. It was also a time in which the city had a strangely isolated air; the streets were shadowy, lamplight was bleak and, nine times out of ten, it was pissing with rain into the bargain. Downtime was the only time certain people could walk the streets.

People like Obegarde.

The wind whistled, rolling bottles along the damp

cobbles and turning over rubbish bins across the city.

On the roof of Karuim's Church an ancient, rust-riddled weathervane moaned in the wind, broke from its support and fell. It landed three inches short of Obegarde.

The investigator flinched. His hearing went fuzzy. A breeze shook the flaps of his dark coat. He looked behind him.

Embedded deep in the cobbles, the weathervane was still taller than a man, its base jutting out of the earth like the hilt of a giant's dagger. A few twisted brackets hung loose. The metal finger that acted as the vane's indicator had folded back on itself. Obegarde noticed, with some small degree of amusement, that it now pointed skyward.

The entrance to the church flew open and a man came hobbling up a stone flight which ascended from the tunnel below. He was elderly, awkward and bespectacled. He wore a ragged suit of leather.

Obegarde squinted through the rain.

'Nasty night,' he said, when the old man was in earshot. He nodded down at the fractured weathervane. 'Narrow escape, there. I was lucky.'

The stranger's scowl suggested that 'lucky' would have meant the investigator being underneath the vane when it fell.

Obegarde extended his hand, waited for about a minute and then withdrew it.

'Good evening,' he began, his mind racing for a suitable ruse. 'I've come about thejdjffkfkdk.'

'What?'

'I said I've come about thejdjjfjdfjfj.'

'I can't hear you. Speak up!'

'Can I go in?'

The old man hobbled up and, to Obegarde's extreme surprise, actually stepped on his toes. When he spoke, uncomfortably close, his breath smelled like rotting flesh.

'Eh? What's that?'

'The church! Can I go into the church?'

'I wouldn't advise it.'

'Why?'

'There's nobody there.'

'Oh. Nobody at all?'

The church acolyte put his head on one side and gave Obegarde a critical stare, practically from inside his own eyeballs.

'You could always talk to Lopsalm,' he said eventually. 'Lopsalm's inside.'

'I thought you said there was nobody inside.'

'Yes, yes, but Lopsalm doesn't count. He's mad, you see. Quite, quite mad. It's *your* funeral.'

Obegarde shoved the old man backward, then took a step forward himself.

'Lopsalm it is,' he said, pushing past. 'Thanks for your help.'

Nine

'Well,' Jimmy said, looking around the haunted expanse of the church roof. 'Where's Grab? I don't see him anywhere.'

Mixer put an experimental foot to the nearest gargoyle, and leaned forward. Then he turned to Jimmy, and gave a shrug.

'Who knows? Maybe he took off.'

'Um . . . right.'

'Thieves are like that, aren't they? Unreliable, I mean.'

'I wasn't.'

'You? You were a thief?'

'Yeah, a while ago now, but I was never very good at it. Not like Grab; he's one of the best.'

Mixer nodded.

'I'm sure he wa— I mean *is*.'

'Right. I wonder where he went.'

'Hmm . . . a mystery.'

'Yeah.' Jimmy wandered across to the edge of the church. 'Cold up here, isn't it?' he ventured, squinting at the gravestones far below. He shivered, shook his head. 'Long way down.'

He started to head over to the small tower containing the church's gargantuan brass bell.

'Well?' he said. 'Let's see this thing chime, then.'

'Indeed,' came the reply. Mixer grinned. 'It'll chime like never before.'

'Without you touching it, o' course,' Jimmy added.

'Of course. Here goes . . .'

The gnome raised his crossbow, and levelled it.

'Ah . . . of course; I should've guessed. You're gonna shoot it, eh?'

Jimmy took a step back.

'No! Stay exactly where you are,' Mixer snapped.

'What? But I'm in the way!'

'Yes, you *are* . . . and so was Grab Dafisful. He had to die too.'

'What? What are you talking about?'

Mixer's grin bled away; he looked suddenly humourless. 'People exceed their use,' he said. 'Take Grab, for instance, he was *extremely* useful, but he also had a very big mouth. You, on the other hand, were simply in the wrong place at the wrong time, and there's just a chance that you know too much. Sorry.'

117

'Hold on a minute! Wrong place? What place? I don't know anything about anything. Are you crazy?'

'No. I'm Mixer. Goodbye, young fool.'

The gnome straightened his crossbow, but just as he was about to fire, something dropped on him. The barrowbird, which had followed the duo religiously from the Ferret and possessed the kind of frenzied death dive which other avians could only dream of, subsequently exploded in a flapping, squawking cacophony.

During the struggle, Jimmy heard a click, and a snap, and then he flew backwards. Fast.

There was a heavy, sonorous clunk as he hit the giant bell.

Then he fell.

Down.

Dowwnn.

Dowwwnnn . . .

Mixer finally managed to shake off the bird, and swiftly realigned his crossbow to bring it down with a bolt. He missed.

The barrowbird soared back into the sky, and flew away.

Ten

The Yowler known as Lopsalm was an undiluted lunatic. At least, he was acting like an undiluted lunatic, and Obegarde suspected the man might be a very good actor. He certainly had the 'crazed priest' archetype down to a tee.

Lopsalm perched atop a communion table in the southern wing of the church, his hands tied behind his back in some sort of supplication ritual, and his small bearded face enclosed in one of the weirdest cowls Obegarde had ever laid eyes on. The cloth monstrosity, apart from its giant hood, had six wayward cords that hung down to cover the priest's ears, and almost extended past his scrawny neck as well.

'Don't you speak to me like that!' he snapped at the investigator. 'How dare you come in here and fire your ignorant questions at me. I, who am of the Chalice.'

'I'm sorry,' said Obegarde. 'I didn't think "You must be Lopsalm?" was a particularly intrusive question.'

'Hah! That's what they all say!'

'Listen—'

'What? Where?'

Obegarde rolled his eyes.

'No, listen to me. I need to ask you a few more intrusive questions. If it helps any, I'll break your neck unless I'm completely satisfied.'

'It's like that, is it?'

'It is.'

Lopsalm scratched his wiry beard.

'Go on then, if you must!' he said.

Obegarde slid an old cloth robe off the table and took a seat beside the priest, who immediately spun around to face him.

'Do you know any gnomes who might work here?'

'Yes and no.'

'Meaning?'

'Well, he comes here. But I've never seen him do any work.'

Obegarde smiled.

'What's his name?'

'Tricky.'

'He's called Tricky the gnome?'

'No, he isn't. I meant it's tricky to remember what his name is. Mixer, I believe, or perhaps Twixer; something of that variety. I've only met him once, and I wasn't too impressed. He's supposed to guard the sacred books.'

'I see. And he doesn't do his job properly?'

'He read more than he guarded. Obsessed with them, he was. He was only here three days when the big one went missing. Haven't seen him since. Less astute minds might consider that a coincidence.'

'But not you,' said Obegarde, with a grin. 'You obviously think he stole it.'

'Not at all. I reckon he was given it.'

'By who?'

Lopsalm shrugged.

'The Lark was fairly fond of him; she spent a lot of time teaching him the ways of Doiley.'

'Doiley?'

'God of Stone; lord immortal and creator of the original rock.'

Obegarde frowned.

'The original rock? What's that?'

'Ha! Ignoramus! It's *the* rock, the rock upon which the foundations of Illmoor were set. The living rock, the rock immortal. The rock that is none other than the great Yowler himself, deep in his thousand-year slumber.'

'Oh, come on. Living rock? You don't honestly believe all that rubbish?'

'It's written in the sacred book; of course I believe it. The sacred book tells no lies. It forecasts a time when Great Yowler will rise. It talks of the second coming of

Doiley, the prophet who'll bring about his resurrection.'

'Second coming? What happened the first time?'

'He didn't quite manage it.'

'Oh, right. I'm sorry to hear that.'

'As are we all. Nevertheless, he will come again. Our Lady Lauris assures us that it is so.'

'Lady—'

'Lauris. We call her the Lark.'

'Ah yes, I remember you mentioning her. She runs the church?'

'No one runs it. We're an autonomous collective; all are equal in the eyes of Yowler. We, that is, myself, the Lark, the behemoth called Moors, and his spindly friend Edwy, are all even-footed. However, the Lark has . . . strong beliefs.'

'Stronger than yours?'

'Stronger than most.'

'And why would this Lark give your gnome the sacred book? More to the point, if you're all equals, why did you let her?'

Lopsalm fiddled with the strange cloth hat.

'I've told you too much already,' he said, without feeling.

'Oh, I don't doubt you've told me everything, yet you've shown me nothing. Clever.'

'Clever? Ha! I've betrayed church secrets, and I've double-crossed friends! I've endangered my standing in the high order, I've put my soul at risk! Indeed, my only consolation will be that you won't live to tell anyone about my indiscretion.'

'Ah, that explains the smile,' Obegarde said. 'You're planning to have me killed.'

'Oh no, Mr Obegarde. You planned to have yourself killed the moment you stuck your nose where it wasn't wanted.'

The investigator peered around him.

'There's nobody here,' he said. 'I could just kill you now . . .'

'You could, but I don't think you will. After all, if you did strike me down, the rest of my order would make it their business to have you sent straight back to Dorley House . . .'

Obegarde froze. 'What?'

'Dorley House, in Spittle? Isn't that the breeding ground where most of your pathetic kind struggle to exist? Isn't that the wretched pit where all the poor, breadline loftwings are forced into servitude? And isn't that why you came to the city, to make enough money so that you might forget your terrible origins?'

The investigator's expression hadn't changed.

'We are Yowlers, Mr Obegarde,' Lopsalm continued. 'We have dirt on everyone and every*thing* in Illmoor. How else do you think we hold sway? In fact, I believe you have an appointment at the palace, tonight?'

'How—'

'Let's see if you can survive the night to keep it.'

Obegarde turned very slowly, and headed for the nearest door. Halfway across the sanctuary he stopped, and looked back at Lopsalm's evil grin.

'This isn't over,' he said.

'Oh it is, Mr Obegarde. I assure you it is.'

Obegarde departed the sanctuary, and didn't look back until he realized that he'd taken the wrong door. Still suffering from the shock of Lopsalm's revealed knowledge, he'd stumbled upon a strangled route through a twisted maze of passageways into the southern wing of the church.

He walked on, and was nearing a possible exit when he spied a thickset ogre standing sentry under three small alcoves. Two of the alcoves, one on either side, contained heavy volumes with elaborate hand-embroidered covers. The middle one was empty.

Obegarde narrowed his eyes, trying to force himself to think clearly.

A dark religion, a sacred book gone, a gnome assassin on the loose and a giant machine camouflaged in a dockyard warehouse. There was some kind of connection there, something he just couldn't put his finger o—

CRASH!

Obegarde looked up as a giant skylight of red and purple stained glass imploded, spewing a rain of needle-sharp shards and a man with an arrow protruding from his shoulder. The latter landed heavily on the thick pile of an altar carpet, rolled on to his back and lay there like a fallen angel. He didn't move.

The ogre sentry had moved with remarkable speed for a creature of its size and, having grabbed a spear from some concealed alcove, was currently edging towards the wounded stranger with a demonic but careful expression on its face.

Luckily, Obegarde reached the man first. He crouched down beside him, checked for a pulse and then wasted no time in yanking the bolt from Jimmy's shoulder.

'*Aaahhhhhhh!!!!!!!!*'

The ogre leapt back, taking up a defensive position in front of the two remaining display cases. It was soon joined by Lopsalm, who hurried in from the main sanctuary, screaming blasphemy on all enemies of the church.

'*Ahhhhhh!!!!!!!Myshoullllllderrdamnlllllt!*' Jimmy cried. He reached up a hand to cover his wound, but Obegarde already had a palm pressed hard against it. The thief felt an alien heat surging through him, strengthening his bones and doubling his resistance to the agony in his shoulder. It lasted no more than a few seconds, and then it was gone. So was the pain.

Jimmy sat up, befuddled and half conscious.

'Th-thanks,' he said. 'Saved me, saved Jimmy. For a bet. Roof. Fell. Gnome. Had a crossbow. Death, dead Jimmy. I'm alive. Is it? Who said that? Where am I, then? Bye.'

He slumped back. Obegarde leaned over him to ensure

that the wound had healed, but a second crossbow bolt thudded into the carpet beside them: unlike the bolt he'd pulled from the stranger, this one was silver-edged. Obegarde glanced up through the serrated hole in the window, and saw the gnome with brass teeth glaring down at him.

Just as a third bolt flew from its housing, Obegarde back-flipped and sprang to his feet. Then, dragging Jimmy's semi-conscious form into the shadows, he bolted from the hall, shoving Lopsalm aside and dodging a (thankfully badly aimed) spear thrown by the ogre sentry.

'Get after him!' Lopsalm screamed, shaking his fists at the distant head of the gnome. 'He'll ruin everything! Well?' He spun around and jabbed an accusatory finger at the ogre. 'What do you think you're doing?'

'Lookin' fo' me spear, guv'nor.'

'Well don't! You see that ragtag scruffian over there? I want you to pick him up an' wring his damn neck!'

'How does I do that, then, guv'nor?'

'I don't know! *You're* the ogre; you figure it out!'

Eleven

It was evening in Dullitch, and the peaceful sleep of the three or four decent citizens still resident in the city was being disturbed by the unmistakable din of crossbow fire.

In the extreme north-east of the church district, two figures sped along the rooftops, leaping gantry-ways and skirting chimney pots as if they were mere markers on a predestined course. You could tell it was a death chase. The big man in front took no measure of his jumps, invariably landed a few inches short of every adjoining rooftop he made for and ended up scrabbling for purchase on the lower slates. Also, the way the pursuer hurried around the weathervanes with his crossbow, instead of lifting the weapon strategically over them, indicated that he was a

127

gnome; a gnome with a grudge (and a crossbow, obviously).

As he ran, Obegarde reflected on his quality of life.

Most of all, he hated the rooftop chases.

Dressed in a flowing coat which seemed as much a peril of the chase as the gnome behind him, he came to an abrupt halt on the summit of the Treasury. Putting a hand to his ribcage, he groaned as his bruises bit him: he hadn't the time to heal. Then, breath freezing on the air, he peered over his shoulder to see whether Mixer had given up. A small explosion just left of his earlobe suggested that, on the contrary, the little bastard was quite prepared to make a night of it. The thought persisting, Obegarde took to his feet again. The gnome followed.

On the narrow ledge atop the Diamond Clock Tower a slate slid away and smashed on to the cobbles far below. Obegarde made the decision to ignore it a little too late and crashed on to the dark, shadowy roof of the History Museum. The impact wasn't flattering; a thousand heroes had made the drop with a lot more style and a lot less fuss, but Obegarde wasn't a hero. He was just a man falling on to a museum roof. There was a difference.

The sky over Dullitch was moving fast; it had already gathered an army of clouds in preparation for the Downtime drizzle. Obegarde scrambled for purchase on a bell's housing as another bolt exploded three inches from his right elbow. Suddenly, looking back across the midnight cityscape, he realized there was nowhere to run. The rooftop of the Steeplejack Inn was too far away and in order to reach Tyrell Tower, he'd have to go back past the Diamond Clock. It was all over then, no question. He closed his eyes and tried to think of a god who might be merciful. None sprang to mind, but then Obegarde wasn't exactly the most religious man in the city; he'd only visited the church once in two years, and that had been to retrieve a stolen crate of Bhorkan Red from the vestry. Shaking himself from his reverie, he tried to review his options. He had about five or six seconds, tops.

Thwack! Another bolt was released in the darkness behind him.

Eyes tightly shut, jaw hardened, Obegarde turned and waited for the agonizing impact of the bolt.

Thunk. The bolt knifed into the roof beside him, splitting the slates into two and dismissing another cracked shard to the cobbles below.

Obegarde swallowed and thanked his stars; as luck would have it, Mixer was aiming badly.

Thwack! A new bolt flew away on the wind.

Obegarde sprang up, eyes darting from side to side as he searched for an easy exit.

Thunk. An arrow this time; the little demon must have changed ammunition; the head bit into Obegarde's chest and he tumbled from the church roof. For a few fleeting seconds, the air whistled in his ears. Then he hit the grass. Hard.

Groaning with the pain of the fall, Obegarde reached a hand to his chest, removed the arrow and tossed it aside. Then he closed his eyes and tried to heal.

Loftwings possess many little idiosyncrasies that separate them from the pure breed. These include the laying-on of hands, a swift recovery from all non-anointed wounds and, if concentration allows, a remarkable ability to play dead.

Silence reigned in the cemetery.

At length, footsteps neared and Mixer loomed into view. Obegarde reflected that for Mixer to loom, you had to be looking up from the ground.

The gnome, crossbow still clenched tightly in his hands, put a foot to the investigator's chest and gave him an experimental nudge. When he got no response, he dropped the weapon, put a hand inside his jerkin and drew out a fistful of red powder. Countless grains poured from between his fingers.

Mixer cast the powder to the floor beside the investigator and mumbled something unintelligible under his breath. There was a sudden eruption of white flame. It was accompanied by a low, resounding hum.

Obegarde allowed his eyelids to part a fraction.

What's this now, he thought. Don't tell me the little freak's a wizard as well as a murdering thug?

The flame died away. In its place stood a woman of striking appearance. She was raven-haired and wearing far fewer clothes than respectability demanded. An air of dark magic surrounded her. She looked down at Mixer's wretched face with something approaching disgust.

'What now?' she demanded.

'It's me, Mixer,' the gnome began. 'I have news.'

'Well?'

'It's the loftwing I was telling you about, Mistress—'

'Ha! That was days ago. You've only just managed to catch up with him? Insufferable! I'm sure I don't know why Lopsalm hired you; that wretched creature might have told the palace *anything* in the time it's taken you to silence him.'

'Yes, Mistress, but I've done it now. My work is over, and all our enemies have been subdued. The thief is a memory, and Master Lopsalm is dealing with his young friend.'

The Lark raised an eyebrow expectantly.

'Good,' she said, slowly. 'But there is still much to do. You have the book?'

'Yes,' Mixer went on, his eyes glazed with uncertainty. 'Shouldn't we tell Master Lopsalm about it?'

'Lopsalm already knows.'

'But, Mistress, you said it was *our* secret.'

'Yes, well . . . just make sure the book is safe.' The Lark smiled. 'As for you, Mixer, I'm still a little confused as to how this "investigator" chanced upon you in the first place.'

'I've been thinking about that, Mistress,' Mixer intoned,

choosing his words carefully. 'Perhaps someone at the palace suspected yo—'

'Me? You dare to suggest that I am the weak link?'

'No, no, of course not, Mistress. Is it not possible that we might have a spy in our midst?'

'A spy?'

'Yes, Mistress. Are you sure the others are reliable?'

The Lark nodded.

'Absolutely,' she said. 'The followers share a common purpose. Besides, Moors and Edwy don't have the imagination required for betrayal.'

'No, Mistress. I'll, er, I'll bring the book to you, then.'

'No! Just hide it. The city MUST NOT find out what we're up to; they still have time to ruin everything we've worked so hard to achieve! So keep that book safe. Also, have the receptacle moved.'

'Wh-what, Mistress? The machine? But it's huge! Where else can—'

'I don't care, but you must let me know *where* it ends up, so that I may aim the ray correctly. Somewhere in the centre of the city would be preferable. A rooftop; I'm assuming you still have the Dust of Levitation?'

'Yes, Mistress.'

'Very good; it took a great deal of bartering to obtain. Communicate with me again when the task is done. Our whole religion is counting on you.'

'Wait, Mistress!'

The image shimmered, but did not disappear.

'Well?'

Mixer shifted uncomfortably.

'What of Moors and Edwy, Mistress? Did they get the lizards to Plunge without incident?'

'Indeed. They are testing the remarkable properties of our scaly little friends right at this moment. Very successfully, I might add. The villagers of Plunge are simply . . . lost for words. Glory awaits.'

Mixer nodded. 'We're almost ready, then!' he hazarded.

'Almost,' the Lark confirmed. 'When the lighthouse lens intensifies our glare, we will be able to fire upon Dullitch. The city will be no more, and our select brotherhood will reign. Just remember to leave AFTER you've moved the machine. If it is discovered, all our hard work will have been in vain.'

A nod; Mixer bowed low.

'I'll not fail you, Mistress,' he said. 'And then, maybe I can join you in Plunge?'

The image in the flame said nothing more; it merely flickered and melted away. Mixer took a moment to stop shaking, then crouched down to retrieve his crossbow. His fingers had just found the handle when Obegarde sprang to his feet and stamped on them.

Twelve

Back in the church, things were not going well for Jimmy Quickstint . . .

The ogre, who had the build (but not the brains) of Groan Teethgrit, had snatched him up by a thatch of hair, spun him around and fastened him in a headlock.

Jimmy kicked out with arms and legs, flailing wildly against the stranglehold which the ogre promptly began to close like a vice.

Using a technique familiar to many stalwart wrigglers of the thieving trade, he allowed himself to go limp and then, when the grip loosened, attempted to slide between the legs of his aggressor and sweep the beast off its feet with a well-aimed tendon kick.

It didn't work.

The ogre, whose legs were as thick as tree trunks,

simply scooped Jimmy up again, snapping him back into the headlock with comparative ease.

However, this time Jimmy was closer to the wall. Releasing a reserve of strength he hadn't previously been aware of, he leapt up with both feet and, placing them flat against the stone, launched himself and the ogre backwards. They flew into the nearest display case which shattered and collapsed under the ogre's weight.

Jimmy was first to his feet. Snatching up a sacred Shindu cannon ball, he swung round with both arms and struck the ogre a glancing blow across the back of its skull. The beast gave a dull grunt, and slumped forward.

Jimmy dropped the cannon ball and fell against the rough stone of the chamber wall, his breath coming in slow gasps. He closed his eyes.

As weeks go, he thought, I've had better. I've been conned by a one-armed thief, pursued by a blasphemous bird, shot at by a gnome with brass teeth, healed by some stranger in a dirty coat and strangled by a dirty great ogre. And it's only Tuesday.

Jimmy took a deep breath. When he opened his eyes again, Lopsalm was right beside him. The priest was displaying a nice warm smile, and a dagger.

'That was a very lucky escape,' he said. 'But now it is time for you to die.'

Jimmy's punch caught the mad priest completely by surprise, and practically knocked him into next week. He followed it up with a second, slightly weaker, but still on target. Lopsalm staggered sideways, and dropped his weapon. Then he turned and fled from the chamber.

'Get after him!' came a familiar squawk.

Jimmy looked up at the barrowbird.

'What?'

'Get after the priest!'

'No way!' he screamed. 'That's the first person who's ever run away from me; I'm not gonna push my luck.'

'If you lose him,' the bird snapped, 'I'll plague you for ever – now get going!'

'Why can't you follow him?'

'I'm gonna see if I can find the gnome and that other bloke. I'll catch up with you afterwards.'

'Promise?'

'Yes! Now, MOVE!!!!!'

Jimmy mustered all his strength and bolted from the church. When he arrived outside, the street was dark. He glanced left and right, trying to distinguish any shape that might be moving faster than those around it. Just as he was about to shrug the whole thing off and make his way back inside, he spotted Lopsalm's floppy hat. It was lying at the mouth of Westcoat Alley, a dim slit which formed a short cut between Dullitch's Merchants' Quarter and the City Cathedral.

Jimmy kicked the hat aside and cautiously entered the alley.

Thirteen

Obegarde had Mixer pinned to the ground.

He rested the edge of the crossbow on the gnome's throat and applied gentle pressure.

'Noooo!' Mixer moaned, eyes streaming with tears. 'Pleeaaasse.'

'Quiet,' snapped Obegarde. 'Now, I'm going to talk and you're going to listen very carefully. Nod if you understand.'

Mixer made a slight inclination with his head but the bolt dug into his throat and drew a thick line of blood.

'OK,' the investigator continued. 'The Lark and her people aren't your friends. They saw you taking an interest in the scriptures and they've brainwashed you.'

Mixer struggled, but Obegarde increased pressure on

the bolt and almost choked the gnome into unconsciousness.

'They've had you running around for them,' he continued. 'Doing all the dangerous work; things *you* could be hanged for. Whereas they, they haven't done anything illegal, at least nothing provable. Now, do you understand what I'm saying?'

The gnome ceased his struggles and appeared, just for a second, to be paying attention.

'You're lying,' he managed, his lips moist with spittle. 'They need me; I'm a vital part of the group. The Mistress and Master Lopsalm will rule, and I'll be at their right hand!'

'Ah. That's why they've left you here, is it?' said Obegarde. 'Here in Dullitch, where everything's going to be turned to stone. From what I heard, those other two cultist clowns are away on the wind and, as for Lopsalm, I'll bet he's already killed that poor lad and spirited himself off to Plunge! Don't look at me like that, you know I'm right. From what I hear, this group of yours are stabbing each other in the back and using you to do it!'

Mixer shook his head, and Obegarde could see all the terrible consequences of his actions dawning on him at once. As Obegarde released his vice-like grip on the crossbow, the gnome brought his hands to his face and wept.

'I wanted to be an assassin,' he sniffed. 'But I failed the initiation, so they banished me to the church as a cleaner.

A cleaner, me! Well, I showed them. Master Lopsalm, and the Lark, they gave me *purpose*. First I kept the sacred book and then, when the thief returned from Grinswood with the lizards . . .'

'Lizards?'

'. . . he knew too much, so I took him down. I only scared the old man; of course, they *wanted* me to kill him.'

'That's enough, I think. You can explain all this to the viscount.'

'You don't understand. I—'

'Come on,' said Obegarde, dragging him up from the floor. 'I'll take you to gaol. The Crown can decide your fate in the morning.' He straightened up, shouldered the crossbow and pushed the gnome in front of him. 'And if you try anything smart, you'll find out why the world hates a loftwing.'

Mixer coughed and managed half a nod.

'Good. Now keep your hands where I can see them.'

He shoved the gnome in the back with his boot and the two of them headed on down the hill.

High in the sky, the barrowbird watched them with considerable interest.

Fourteen

The alley was wreathed in shadow.

Jimmy Quickstint picked his way, catlike, between crumpled bins and bulging rubbish sacks that spilled their contents from gaping wounds. Occasionally he would stand stock-still and listen for the slightest hint of movement ahead. Then, detecting nothing, he would move on much as before, hands bunched into fists for the attack he expected at any moment.

Then he saw Lopsalm. The mad priest was a tiny speck at the furthest end of the alley, about to cross into Cathedral Street.

Slowly at first, then beginning to pick up speed, Jimmy moved faster and faster until he was hurtling headlong after the priest, arms pumping and legs threatening to strike every inch of the way.

What am I doing NOW? he thought. Eleven o'clock at night and, when I should be tucked up in bed, I'm chasing a religious lunatic down a blind alley at the request of a damn pigeon. I must be mad; there's no other explanation. Never mind, I've nearly caught him. Oh look, he's going into the cathedral grounds. I wonder if Jed's working tonight?

Fifteen

The loftwing branch of the vampire family was characterized by its breathtaking reflexes, which were described by some anthropologists as 'so fast as to be almost anticipatory'. Mixer, on the other hand, was desperate, and occasionally desperation carries an amazing ability to turn back the odds.

They were approaching Dullitch City Gaol when the gnome made his move. Obegarde, who'd had the nose of the crossbow jammed into Mixer's back since the moment he'd hoisted him off the cobbles, was beginning to relax. The gaol loomed into view at the end of the street, and manholes aside, there was simply nowhere for the little gnome to go.

Then, without the slightest physical indication, Mixer took off like a torpedo . . . *towards* the gaolhouse. Wary and not a little baffled, Obegarde rocketed after him, slowing a little when he realized the gnome was on a collision course with the gaol's immense barred door. But Mixer knew exactly what he was doing.

'Hey, stop him!' Obegarde screamed at the sentries when he saw the little gnome squeeze himself *between* the bars and disappear into the darkness beyond.

The two guards on duty began to stumble about in confusion, partly befuddled and partly bemused at the fact that someone had just forced their way *into* the building. Mixer evaded them with consummate ease, sliding between their clumsy limbs and leading them a merry dance along the gloomy corridors of the gaol.

Obegarde arrived at the entrance to the gaolhouse, crashing into the giant door and hammering on the bars until his knuckles bled.

'Let me in, you fools! He's going to get away!'

'Leave this to us, citizen!' the guards bellowed back. 'We have everything under control.'

'Like hell you do! LET ME IN!'

There was a lengthy pause, and the gate began to trundle sideways. Obegarde grabbed at the retreating bar and propelled himself inside. Unfortunately, he then ran smack bang into the one person in Dullitch he tried passionately to avoid: Quartermaster Alan Sorrow.

'Obegarde, what a lovely surprise; and where do you think *you're* going?'

Sorrow wasn't a well-liked man in Dullitch. In fact, he

was positively loathed. This was something he simply couldn't fathom, for, being one of the four quartermasters, he considered himself highly respectable. Obegarde, on the other hand, he regarded as a hopeless piece of street scum. This didn't worry the loftwing unduly, as the feeling was mutual.

'Alan,' he said, breathlessly, 'you've got to let me pass. There's a gnome on the loose in there.'

'Yes, it seems so,' Sorrow agreed, putting his head on one side and listening as a hundred pairs of feet responded to the unmistakable din of the gaolhouse alarm gong. 'Do you have any idea why that is?'

'Yes,' the loftwing managed. 'I brought him in. Now can I—'

'Hold your horses, Obegarde. My men will handle it. What's the charge?'

'Um . . . murder, assault, possible theft, conspiracy to endanger the city, er, you name it . . .'

'I see. Nice of you to let him go, then.'

'What? I *didn't* let him go.'

'Then would you like to explain what he's doing running loose around my gaolhouse?'

'He escaped.'

'Terrific. Well, we'll handle it from here. We are, after all, *professionals*.'

Obegarde snorted. 'You're a bunch of incompetents,' he muttered.

'What was that?'

'I said, you're a bun—'

'Yes, I heard you the first time; I just wanted to see if a bloodsucker like yourself had the bottle to repeat it. I have to confess, I'm shocked.' He stepped forward, ushering Obegarde into the street, and motioned for the great gates to be closed behind him.

'You're coming with me,' he said, flatly.

'Where?'

'The palace. I understand Lord Curfew's secretary wants to see you, though I can't think why the palace would employ a *freelance* when they've got us.'

Sixteen

The ancient gates barring entrance to the grounds of Dullitch Cathedral creaked ominously in the wind; the chains that usually constricted them had been severed. The grounds were wreathed in shadow.

'Watch your back here, boy,' said the barrowbird, landing on the iron gatepost. 'I reckon that Lopsalm could be a tricky customer.'

'Thanks,' said Jimmy, wretchedly. 'I'll keep that in mind when he's beating my brains out with a candlestick.'

'No need for sarcasm, I'm just trying to help.'

'Thanks.' Jimmy spotted a shade slipping between two stone monuments and crouched down to hide himself in the long-neglected grass. A few seconds later the shade emerged and, looking both ways, nipped behind another statue. It was definitely Lopsalm; the little priest's pathetically scrawny form gave him away.

'Out of his mind,' muttered the barrowbird. 'That's one of the requirements of being a priest, if you ask me. Start a bloke off wearing a dress and sooner or later things are bound to go wrong.'

'You may have stumbled upon something there,' said Jimmy.

'What's that?'

'Well, wizards wear robes and most of them go bad. There was one up in, there was one, er, I don't remember . . .' Jimmy trailed off. He knew that he must be pretty scared, subconsciously, because he'd started talking for the sake of talking, and that was always a sure sign of trouble.

He kept himself low to the ground, and pulled himself along on his stomach. The damp from the grass seeped into his clothes and, somewhere behind him in the darkness, a flapping indicated that the barrowbird had moved skyward to get a better view of the proceedings.

Lopsalm was clearly visible now, and his destination was equally obvious. The scabby little priest was heading for the hulking mass of the cathedral. He broke into a run and had almost cleared the first flight of steps when he tripped, and fell.

The barrowbird flapped furiously.

'Now! Quick, while the bugger's down!'

Jimmy bolted. Running faster than he'd ever run before, he cleared bushes and gravestones with jumps that would've ruined a shorter man for life. Lopsalm was getting to his feet when the gravedigger cannoned into him. The two men rolled on the ground, raining blows on each other in the familiar fashion of men who've never fought before and are trying to remember how their fathers had told them to bunch a fist.

Jimmy scored the first 'oof', but spent too long congratulating himself and got caught across the chin with a brass knuckleduster Lopsalm had seemingly produced from thin air.

'The Holy Hand of Yowl!' yelled the priest, his grin ethereal in the moonlight. 'How it striketh thee down!'

Jimmy brought up a knee and, more from luck than judgement, connected with the man's most sacred relics.

'The, er, Gravedigger's Thrust of Doom,' he barked back. 'How it makes your eyes water!'

Lopsalm creased up and collapsed, something that Jimmy mistakenly interpreted as licence for a breather. He struggled to his feet, took a step back and tripped over the edge of a gravestone. When he managed to struggle up again, the priest had vanished.

'You cloth-eared sot!' squawked the barrowbird, flapping on the wind. 'You shouldn't have taken your eyes off him!'

Jimmy groaned. 'Did you see where he went?'

'Yeah; in there.'

The cathedral loomed large. Jimmy hoped it didn't look as bad on the inside, but something about the expressions of the gargoyles suggested the architect had been working on a theme of unimaginable terror.

'Well, here goes nothing,' he said, and sprinted off, the barrowbird close behind him.

Seventeen

An ear-splitting scream echoed through the palace corridors. There was a lengthy pause, then . . .

'WHAT IS THE MEANING OF THIS DISRUPTION?' the viscount boomed. He'd been somewhat taken aback when Secretary Spires had rushed into his private chambers (once again without knocking) accompanied by a bedraggled stranger in a dirty overcoat. He made a mental note to execute his chamber guards, assuming he could find them.

Obegarde, still panting heavily from the night's exertions, took a step back and collapsed into one of the palace's hard marble chairs. Spires was less keen to be silent, and stood at the edge of Curfew's desk, his hands visibly shaking.

'Now,' the viscount began. 'I'm sure you're here on the

most urgent of business, but still, I'd appreciate it if you at least made an attempt to announce yourself. These intrusions really are most . . .' He trailed off as he saw the secretary's expression. 'What is it, man?'

'I have vital news, Excellency.'

'What news? Who is *this* fellow?'

'First things first, Master. The young lady you asked me to trace – I searched the palace for info, asked every employee. I turned up nothing.'

'Unfortunate . . .'

'Yes, but then I spoke to the Yowlers.'

'You did WHAT? Without my permission! You imbecile! You do realize that anything you say reflects on me? Do you know how many Yowler groups there are in this city? Moreover, do you know how many Yowlers there are in *this quarter* of the city? If you've compromised my posit–'

'Don't worry, Excellency! Please, don't worry! The news isn't as bad as we think–'

'Oh, it's bad all right,' Obegarde interrupted.

'Quiet! You'll get your turn, whoever you are.'

'I'm just saying–'

'Well, don't. Let him finish. Go on, Spires.'

The secretary passed a set of parchments to the viscount.

'I think you should take a look at these profiles, Excellency.'

Curfew studied the scrolls, his cheek twitching as his eyes progressed down each page.

'Moors, Edwy, the Lark? Who *are* these people?'

'A breakaway section of the Yowlers, Excellency.'

'How breakaway, exactly? Breakaway as in still tied to or breakaway as in totally defunct? I don't want to end up murdered in my bed—'

'They're total outcasts, Excellency; I assure you. They deserted the main order last year to start up on their own; the ruling brotherhood say they won't have anything to do with them because they're all mad.'

Curfew swallowed a few times, wiping his brow with the back of his hand. Spires slowly took back the parchments and continued.

'Moors, Edwy and Lopsalm are all ex-priests from the order. We think the fourth member, the one known as the Lark, might be our girl Lauris.'

Curfew snatched the parchments back, and rifled through them.

'Hmm . . . these aren't very good. Apart from the fact that this *Moors* is supposed to be grossly obese, we don't have an awful lot to go on; most of these pictures are drawn in crayon.'

'Yes, Excellency – our artist *was* working from a few vague descriptions. But, wait! There's more. The Yowlers say that one of their grand churches was recently sold to this Lopsalm character for a sum referred to as considerable.'

'Let me guess: Karuim's?'

'Precisely, Excellency: used to be the temple of origins, didn't it?'

Curfew bristled. 'But that's next door, for goodness' sake! We can storm it.'

'Unfortunately not, Excellency. The church is on Yowler land, and even though they're opposed to the new order, we'll incur their considerable wrath if we thunder right in there with no religious jurisdiction.'

'Absolutely, absolutely. We don't want that kind of trouble . . . you'll have to think of something else. Where does this fellow come in?'

The loftwing stepped forward, and gave a reluctant bow.

'This is Mr Obegarde, Excellency, the investigator we hired to track Lauris.'

Curfew nodded.

'Ah yes; last I heard you were chasing after a gnome who worked as a cleaner at the church?'

'Oh, he's a cleaner all right,' Obegarde conceded. 'He's also an assassin, a thief, a conspirator and only the gods know what else.'

'Definitely a member of the group, then?'

'Oh yes.'

'Did you catch him?'

'I did, and I took him to the City Gaol.'

'He's there now?'

'I doubt it.'

'Oh?'

'He got away from me in the gaolhouse. Sorrow's men might catch him, but I wouldn't build your hopes up . . .'

The viscount caressed his eyelids with a thumb and a forefinger.

'I see,' he said, sadly. 'And do we have any idea, absolutely *any idea*, what all this is about?'

'Not really,' Obegarde admitted. 'All I've got is a few fractured facts from eavesdropping and a very dodgy confession from our little friend. What I do know is this: there's a machine in a warehouse down at the harbour, it's big, it's mean and it's definitely a vital part of whatever this group has planned. If we can do a demolition job on the cursed thing, my bet is we'd be putting a major dent in their plans. It's in Warehouse Six.'

Curfew nodded.

'Spires,' he began, gripping the arms of his chair so hard that his fingernails turned white, 'I want you to take all available guards and destroy this machine. Do it quickly. Do it now. I'll come along for good measure. Anything else that might help?'

'Possibly,' Obegarde said, when Spires had hurried from the room. 'The Lark has gone to Plunge.'

'Plunge? But that's miles away. Have you any idea why?'

'No, but she had a thief steal some lizards from a forest up north, and the gnome killed him. Now her minions have them; as far as I can make out they're en route to rendezvous with her.'

'In Plunge?'

'Yes. Whatever she's planning, I'm guessing these lizards are an integral part of it.'

At that moment, Spires returned. He stood in the corridor, fully armoured and gasping for air.

'The men are ready, Excellency,' he said.

Eighteen

Having shinned up a sheer brick wall in the nave of the cathedral, Jimmy Quickstint vaulted over the edge of a balcony and landed, on all fours, in the dark antechamber beyond.

'Stuff this,' he spat at the barrowbird who flew over the balcony to land beside him. 'He could be anywhere.'

'Just stay alert, boy. I'll keep watch for you.'

Jimmy squinted into the gloomy shadows cast by the cathedral's innards. He nipped over to crouch beside a heavy iron pipe that ran from floor to ceiling, and put an ear to the outer shell.

'What're you doing, boy?'

'Shhh! It's an old thief trick.'

'You were a thief?'

'BE QUIET!'

Jimmy strained to listen; somewhere far off in the gargantuan sanctuary, he heard the unmistakable click of a door closing.

'Well?' squawked the barrowbird. 'Getting anything?'

'Mmm . . . I think he's downstairs.'

'Straight up? How can you tell?'

Jimmy tapped the pipe indicatively and raised an eyebrow.

'A door closed,' he said.

'Ah. How do you know it was him, though?' asked the barrowbird. 'There must be folk working here, place this size: bishops, canon, cardinals and the like.'

'Cathedral's abandoned,' Jimmy snapped. 'Didn't you see the chain on the gates. No one comes here now, not since the Yowlers outlawed other religions. The grounds 're still used for burials, but that's about it.'

The catacombs beneath Dullitch Cathedral were legendary.

Stretching for half a mile in every direction, they linked up with the city's equally legendary sewer system. Rumour suggested that black elves wandered the subterranean waterways, but no one had survived long enough to prove it.

Jimmy, the barrowbird perched jauntily on his shoulder, squinted ahead. The passageway he'd happened upon culminated in a T-junction and the figure lingering there was definitely not a black elf. Jimmy couldn't be sure, but he hoped it was the rogue Yowler priest.

'Hey, you! Stop in the name of, er—'

'Jort,' said the barrowbird.

'Yes! Stop in the name of Jort!'

The figure at the end of the tunnel paused, shook a fist in Jimmy's direction and disappeared left.

'Who's Jort?' said the gravedigger, hurrying after him.

'Powerful god.'

'Really? I've never heard of him.'

'No, well, I can't say I'm totally shocked. He doesn't get much publicity in these parts.'

Jimmy nodded. 'Who does?'

They pursued Lopsalm to the end of the tunnel, where a door gaped open to reveal an ancient and precipitously steep staircase. Footsteps were barely audible some six or seven flights up.

'Where d'you reckon they go?' asked the barrowbird.

Jimmy shrugged.

'A fair way, I imagine. Judging from the echo, they might even lead to the cathedral roof.'

'Incredible! The architect who built this place must've been out of his tree.'

'Or religious,' Jimmy added. 'In practice, it seems to amount to the same thing.'

The stairs went on and on. Jimmy counted more than four hundred before they ran out on him. There was an old wooden trapdoor in the ceiling, and nowhere else to go.

He took a second to sniff the air, and cautiously lifted

the door. A blanket of rain splattered on his face.

Thunder rumbled overhead.

The barrowbird took off.

Jimmy padded out on to the flat expanse of the roof.

Unfortunately, before he could begin the hunt, Lopsalm dropped from a gargoyle's outstretched wing and clubbed him on the back of the neck with a candlestick.

Lopsalm stepped forward, his lips curled in a terrible smile.

He reached down and snatched hold of Jimmy's leg. Then he dragged the gravedigger into the centre of the cathedral roof and, after a few minutes spent observing his handiwork, produced a mini-bow from the depths of his robe.

'Your death will be . . . interesting,' he muttered. 'Certainly not fast, but enjoyable nevertheless.'

Jimmy was beginning to come round, his vision clearing to reveal the demonic features of Lopsalm and also, beyond, a tiny black speck descending from the sky at an alarming rate. But the priest had noticed Jimmy's gaze wandering.

Lopsalm stepped back and squinted up at the sky, mere seconds before the barrowbird came into view. He raised the mini-bow and fired. The arrow arced into the air, striking the bird with such force that it flew backwards a few feet before it began to plummet.

But the bird's diversion had bought Jimmy a few valuable seconds. The gravedigger catapulted himself to his feet, kicked the bow from Lopsalm's grasp and shoved the priest backwards, hard.

Lopsalm faltered and tried to right himself, but it was too late. Jimmy lashed out with a fist and sent the Yowler priest hurtling dangerously close to the edge of the cathedral roof. Lopsalm managed to snatch at a protruding slate and save himself but, as he struggled to regain his footing, the momentum of his impromptu flight overtook him.

Jimmy saw his chance.

He leapt, landing with a well-placed boot in the middle of Lopsalm's chest.

The collision was fast and furious. Lopsalm gasped and toppled backwards, flapping his arms furiously in a last-ditch attempt to save himself.

A scream erupted.

And Lopsalm fell.

For a moment, there was silence.

Jimmy Quickstint, hunkered down on all fours and bleeding at the mouth, peered out over the edge of the roof. Through a blanket of fine rain, he glimpsed something very messy spread out on the steps below. The tally of Yowler followers in Dullitch, he reflected, had just gone down by one.

Jimmy sighed, and his heart slowed. He stared down dispassionately at the corpse, before the strangled cries of the barrowbird shook him from his reverie. He struggled to attain a standing position and made his way over the damp tiles to where the bird lay squawking weakly, the arrow still protruding from its puffy breast.

'Awwk!'

'Be quiet. Let me pull it out.'

'It's no good, mate. I'm a goner.'

'Nonsense. One sharp tug and—'

'I'm telling you, boy, it's fatal. I've had it.'

'Where did you get such a negative attitude?'

'No joke. I'm-I'm-I'm-'

There was a sudden, pulse-stopping pause. Then a flash of lightning arced from the sky and struck the barrowbird. Surrounded by a shimmering wave of electric energy, it squawked, shuddered, and began to change shape.

Jimmy looked on, open-mouthed, as the distortion took on the recognizable form of a small and very wiry old man. He was wearing a tattered piece of cloth stretched (rather to its limits) into a sort of nappy arrangement.

Thunder rumbled. Erratic lightning flashed again, even more brilliantly than before, and the skies darkened.

'What the hell is this?' shouted Jimmy. 'Who are you, some kind of metamorphic wizard?'

'No, mate,' said the old man, his breath beginning to fail. 'Never gone much on wizardry, myself.'

'Necromancer?'

'N-no.'

'Sorcerer?'

'N-n-no.'

'A god then, I'm guessing.'

The old man shrugged.

'No, th-though I was cursed by the disciples of a particularly watchful one.'

Jimmy's eyes narrowed.

'So you're just a mortal man who annoyed a god?'

'Ha! Y-y-you g-got it.

'Are you going to die?'

'Y-yes, but not before you promise me something.'

Jimmy's concerned expression drained away; it was replaced by an apprehensive twitch.

'It doesn't involve another roof, does it? I'm actually pretty terrified of heights.'

'L-L-Lopsalm's n-not alone. M-make sure you g-g-get the others. T-t-terrible doooom.'

'What? How *can* I? I don't even know who the others are, damn it! These are the Yowlers we're talking about. There might be hundreds of them!'

'P-p-p-promise.'

'No . . .'

'P-p-p-p-promise.'

'No!'

'P-p-p-p-p-promise.'

'NO!'

'P-p-p—'

'ALL RIGHT I PROMISE!!!!!!!! But, I can't—'

The old man died.

'Damn you!' Jimmy screamed. 'Now I've made a promise I can't damn well keep. You crafty, vindictive, decrepit old . . . corpse!'

As if in reply, the skies opened up and he was pelted with hailstones. Throwing his arms up over his head, he made a valiant turn against the rain and out over the wide, statue-smothered roof. With any luck he'd be able to get to the trapdoor before the gods stoned him to death; he certainly wouldn't be taking the short cut down.

Nineteen

The frenzied activity of the city guard had brought most of the inhabitants of the harbour district out into the streets.

Viscount Curfew, who'd decided to personally oversee the destruction of the machine in Warehouse Six, stood at the rear of the demolition team, shouting orders and offering the occasional boon of encouragement when a particularly big chunk crashed to the ground. The team, who'd obviously been informed of the machine's imminent threat to the city, were hacking away at its various extremities like men possessed, while an ogre-led brute force (employed at the very last minute by an inspired guard sergeant) made light work of any bits the main team couldn't handle. Giant, angled mirrors came crashing to the floor, while various tubular wooden arms containing even more reflective barriers were ripped off and soundly stamped into dust. Curfew prayed to the gods of justice that those responsible surfaced quickly.

Obegarde and Spires mingled among the growing assembly of late night harbour workers, assuring them that there was nothing to worry about and urging them to return to their business.

'It's a routine inspection,' Spires explained to one bystander, while Obegarde, bluffing with greater success, offered another the explanation that 'His lordship got a letter of complaint from the Harbour Master; we don't know who owns the thing, but it's taking up far too much room.'

As was usually the case in Dullitch, the crowd ended up squabbling among themselves and generally forgot what all the fuss had been about in the first place.

Curfew sidled up to his secretary.

'Well, it's done, Spires,' he whispered. 'We've managed to destroy the machine *and* avoid any repercussions from the Yowlers.'

'You think so, milord?'

'Absolutely. They can't interfere while they're trying to disassociate themselves from this breakaway group. All we have to do now is round up the stragglers and haul them in. At least, all those still at large in Dullitch.'

'Very good, Excellency.'

'I want you to send a group of guards to Karuim's

Church. As soon as anyone sets foot outside that building, I want them arrested.'

'Yes, Excellency.'

Curfew turned back to face the demolition squad. 'The most important thing would seem to be the machine and, thankfully, we've annihilated that.' He pointed over at the massed heap of rubble. 'DUMP IT ON A BARGE AND SHIP IT OUT!' he screamed at the city guards. 'You've done a good job, men. A very good job!'

As the crowd dispersed, Obegarde spotted Alan Sorrow and managed to catch up with the Quartermaster before his guards vacated the warehouse.

'Yes, what is it now?'

'Did you catch the gnome?'

'Now, listen—'

Obegarde made a frantic grab for the Quartermaster.

'DID YOU OR DIDN'T YOU?' he yelled, as three of Sorrow's subordinates wrenched him away from their commander.

'No, we didn't,' Sorrow fumed, shoving Obegarde back into the impromptu wall formed by his men. 'In fact, I very much doubt if there even *was* a frigging gno— Lord Curfew, what can we do for your Excellency?'

The guard group parted to admit the viscount, Spires waddling along after him like an affectionate puppy.

'Is there a problem, here?' the viscount said.

'No problem, Lordship, but this fellow here is getting to be a damn—'

'Hero?'

'Well, n—'

'City defender? Champion of the people? Choose your words wisely, Master Sorrow. You have the gnome known as Mixer in custody?'

Sorrow looked to his men for support but, unsurprisingly, they had all mooched away.

'Um . . . not exactly, Lordship.'

'I assume you're working on it.'

'Absolutely, Lordship.'

Obegarde shook his head, and marched from the warehouse. 'As I said before, I wouldn't hold my breath.'

Twenty

Obegarde was quite surprised when, returning from the harbour district, he ran straight into the ragbag youth from the church. He was even more surprised when the stranger saw *him*, turned on his heel and fled off up the lane.

'Hey, you! Wait there!'

The loftwing gave chase, hurtling over the cobbles and leaping the odd rubbish bin strategically kicked in his path. Eventually he cornered the stranger in an alley between Winding Way and Birch Street.

'My name's Jimmy Quickstint,' Jimmy bleated. 'I'm just a gravedigger. I'm not a thief, or an assassin, or a priest or a curate or anything to do with Yowler. I don't know how I got involved in all this – just leave me alone!'

Obegarde grinned, and nodded.

'Jareth Obegarde, investigator; and you're not going anywhere until you tell me why the gnome tried to kill you.'

'I don't know why!' said Jimmy, exasperatedly. 'He just *did*. He killed Grab too.'

'Grab?'

'Yeah, Grab Dafisful; mind you, that was probably due to stealin' for those cultists. That was why the bird was after him in the first place.'

'What's this? A bird? I think you'd better tell me everything from the beginning.'

Jimmy collapsed into a snivelling heap on the floor.

'I was afraid you'd say that,' he said. 'But I'm tired, I'm so tired I can barely stand up.'

Obegarde helped the gravedigger to his feet.

'I think I know somewhere you'd get a really good night's sleep,' he said. 'You can tell me all about your adventures on the way.'

So they walked, and they talked. At least, Jimmy talked and, apart from the occasional 'What's that?' and the more frequent 'You're having me on', Obegarde listened.

Twenty-One

Elsewhere in the city, Duke Modeset was nodding off to sleep in his new room when the window rattled. He turned over and tugged on the mangy rag that the Innkeeper had assured him was a blanket.

A wolf howled, and the window rattled.

Modeset frowned, opened one eye and peered over the edge of the blanket. Outside, the twin moons kept up their night-time vigil. He couldn't see anything beyond the barrier so, hugging his knees for warmth, he tried to drift off again.

An owl hooted, and the windows rattled.

It's that rotten bastard of an innkeeper, he thought. I bet there was a wedge for that window and he's had it removed . . . out of spite.

He sat up in bed, gaze fixed on the glass as the

Downtime rains began their vigorous bombardment of the city.

The window rattled.

Modeset sighed, leaped out of bed and padded across the room. He didn't know what he expected to see, but it'd be fair to say that a vampire hanging from the gutter probably wouldn't have made his top ten.

Inconceivable, he thought. Forty-seven rooms and he's still gone and found me.

The window was opened, and Obegarde barrelled into the room. He did a neat little forward roll on the floorboards, stood up, patted himself down, then spun around. Modeset thought he looked bigger in the half-light of the moons.

'Hello again,' he said, not unpleasantly.

'Yes, indeed,' said Modeset. 'Good of you to visit. Er . . . how's everything going?'

Obegarde shrugged.

'So so,' he said. 'Nice room, this. Classy furniture.'

'Yes, indeed,' said the duke. 'I expect you're wondering how I persuaded the Innkeeper to part with it?'

'No,' said Obegarde, taking a seat on the edge of the bed. 'Actually, I was wondering why you didn't open the window sooner.'

Modeset smiled humourlessly.

'Now just look here, I've said I'll go and see this Vrunak chap. What more do you want?'

'I just wanted to tell you what I've found out.'

Modeset folded his arms. He looked nonplussed.

'I thought you didn't want me to stick my nose in,' he said. 'And then, as I recall, you almost broke it.'

'Yeah, OK, but you might as well help now you're involved.'

'What? I'm not involved! Not one bit.'

Obegarde straightened himself up. He was well over six feet tall and, as far as Modeset could see, his wide chest didn't contain one ounce of flab.

'You're involved because I say you're involved,' he began. 'If you wanted to stay out of the case you shouldn't have broken into the warehouse.'

Modeset threw up his arms.

'I didn't break into the warehouse, you idiot! I already told you what happened.'

'Mmm. A likely story, and you're still going to Vrunak's house tomorrow. Now, listen – oh, damn! I almost forgot.'

Obegarde hurried over to the window, stuck his head outside and motioned down towards the street. A few minutes later, a figure fell, puffing and wheezing, through the window and on to the floor of the room.

Obegarde gave Modesct a friendly grin.

'I believe you know Jimmy Quickstint,' he said.

When the duke had stopped shouting, Obegarde proceeded to tell him about Lopsalm, the second coming of Doiley, the missing book and Jimmy's involvement with the barrowbird. Modeset eventually got to sleep at a quarter to seven.

Twenty-Two

In the front garden of a small cottage on Royal Road, a bush rattled in an extremely suspicious manner.

Jimmy Quickstint, who had circled the building twice, leapt the low front wall to crouch beside it.

'There's nobody about,' he said. 'The kitchens are deserted, and I've had a squint in all the windows on the first floor. Why don't you just go and knock?'

Modeset stuck his head out of the biggest bush.

'This is a very delicate matter,' he said. 'I'd thank you not to interfere beyond surveillance suggestions.'

'It's up to you, Duke Modeset. I'm just trying to help.'

'Well, don't.'

Modeset was getting sick and tired of Jimmy; he'd already sent Flicka back to the inn because of her constant nagging – now he had to put up with the gravedigger's irritating chatter.

Jimmy yawned.

'At least you can tell Obegarde we've checked the place out,' he said. 'There's obviously no one here.'

'Please be quiet.'

'Fine, fine.'

Modeset got to his feet and stepped out of the bush, shoving the gravedigger aside. He marched up the garden path and hammered on the door.

'Mr Vrunak? Mr Vrunak! My name is Modeset. I wondered if I could have a quick chat with you.'

Nothing.

Modeset put an ear to the door and listened, but he couldn't hear any movement from within.

'Kick it down,' Jimmy urged. 'No one'll hear.'

'Shh! There must be another way.'

'What d'you mean? A key under the welcome mat?'

Modeset looked down. There was no welcome mat.

'Probably not,' he admitted. 'I'll try the flowerpot instead.'

He reached down and lifted the pot, but there was nothing underneath it. He then tried running a hand under the wooden overhang at the foot of the door, working a finger into the keyhole and, finally, trying to get his fingernails around the edge of a fractured pane.

'Pity,' said Jimmy, when he'd given up. 'Full marks for effort, though.'

Modeset shrugged.

'Well, I've done what he asked me to do,' he said, knowing deep down that it wouldn't be enough. 'What more can he reasonably expect? It's not my fault if the man's not in.'

'Exactly. We *should* go; I mean, we can hardly wait here all day.'

'That's right! I'm not waiting around like some . . . peasant. Vrunak's out; well that's just too bad. Obegarde can come back when it's dark; do the job himself.'

'Yep. Sounds fair.'

'Right.'

'Let's be off to meet him, then. Shall we?'

'Fine.'

'Great.'

The duke headed back up the garden path, Jimmy in tow. They were passing a dense thicket when Modeset tripped on a crack in the paving stones. He went down hard and Jimmy, who hadn't managed to anticipate anything from the Dafisful incident onwards, landed in a crumpled heap beside him.

Modeset groaned. He was bruised, his pride still ached and he felt awful.

He tried to get to his feet but Jimmy, suddenly alert, dragged him back down again and pulled him off the path. They rolled over one another before Modeset wrestled an arm free.

'Let go! What's with you?'

'Shh . . . there's someone coming.'

Still flat to the ground, the duo watched as Vrunak's gate creaked open. A straggly and bedraggled man stepped into the garden, closed the gate behind him and carried on up the path.

'It's the gnome from last night,' Jimmy whispered.

Mixer had reached Vrunak's front door, where he made straight for the flowerpot. When the key was found to be missing, he looked both ways and then flew into a rage, shaking his fists at the windows, kicking the door and cursing Vrunak's name in a variety of different languages. Modeset thought that he heard the words 'treacherous old git' mentioned more than once.

Eventually the gnome seemed to come to a decision and made his way around the side of the cottage.

'Should we try and capture him, d'you think?' Modeset ventured.

'Nah, I doubt we could. I know *I* couldn't.'

Modeset looked affronted.

'Speak for yourself, coward,' he snapped. 'I've had one fight already this week, so I—'

'Did you win?'

'Um . . . yes, sort of. In fact, the other chap didn't get a single blow in.'

'Really? You're that good?'

'No, actually I ran away before he could react. Now come on!'

The duke nodded towards the house, but his determination was interrupted.

'Oi!' Jimmy whispered. 'Get down! He's comin' back.'

Mixer, apparently unsuccessful in his quest to gain an illicit entrance to the cottage, emerged from the side of the building and stomped back up the path. When he reached the gate he took one last look at the house, spat on the ground and headed off along Royal Road.

'We could follow him,' said Jimmy, doubtfully.

Modeset looked astonished.

'Follow him?' he exclaimed. 'In order to achieve what, exactly?'

The gravedigger shrugged.

'To see where he goes, of course. Why else would you follow somebody?'

'No,' snapped Modeset. 'I've got a much better idea. We split up, and *you* go after the gnome. Then you can come and find me at the inn.'

'Why me?'

'You suggested it.'

'So?'

'Just get a move on. Quick, before you lose him.'

Twenty-Three

It was early evening in Dullitch, and the Diamond Clock on Crest Hill struck six.

Flicka, who had been sent on to the old, half-rotted balcony of the inn to watch out for Jimmy Quickstint, whistled a tune that provoked jeers from the weary market traders.

The Innkeeper had guided Modeset into the basement of the Steeplejack Inn to wake Obegarde.

The duke sat on the bottom step of the basement staircase, fidgeting nervously and trying to keep his eyes off the coffin on which the loftwing had placed his early evening pick-me-up: freshly squeezed beetroot juice.

'Thins the blood,' he explained when he saw Modeset's expression. 'Have to keep healthy, don't you?'

Modeset shifted his buttocks to the top of a small wine

barrel, but after a few minutes looked about ready to give up and sit on the floor instead.

'So we're waiting on Jimmy,' said Obegarde, savouring the juice with poorly concealed glee. Modeset had already filled him in on their expedition to Vrunak's house.

'I've been researching the Grinswood,' Obegarde continued. 'And I fear we don't know the half of it, yet.'

'Oh?'

'According to Jimmy, the barrowbird said it was a servant of the forest. That would also make it a servant of the Dark Trinity. "Watchers",' Obegarde explained, holding up a hand to stop Modeset interrupting. 'Those that make sure everything stays as it is, more or less.'

'OK. And these watchers sent the bird when Jimmy's friend took the lizards, correct?'

'As far as I can make out, yes. But the point is, this all started up because our city's lunatic fringe group wanted 'em; we now know *why*.'

There was a knock on the basement door and Flicka poked her head around it.

'A friend of yours,' she said.

Jimmy staggered into the basement.

'Any luck?' said Obegarde, offering the gravedigger some beetroot juice which he quite rightly refused.

'Yeah, he went home,' Jimmy said. 'Lives in a hovel west of the palace; a right old slum. I've seen better windows in a doll's house. Rump Lane, it's called; I waited till he went out before I came back. Maybe we can search the place.'

Obegarde got to his feet.

'Right. Who's with me?' he said.

No one made a sound.

'I'll assume that's just myself and the duke, then.'

He glared at Modeset who looked about ready to explode and then simmered down considerably.

'I'm up for it,' said Flicka.

Jimmy realized he was on his own, and groaned.

Twenty-Four

Rump Lane was one of the first roads to be built when Dullitch laid its foundations on the ash-lands of Illmoor. Now, more than two hundred years later, it looked about the same.

'What a dump,' said Obegarde.

'Absolute abomination,' said Modeset, looking at Flicka in case she felt like mentioning the kennels.

'Used to rent a little place along here,' Jimmy muttered. 'It was all right. Bit of damp in the walls but nothing worth condemning it over.'

Obegarde put a finger to his lips.

'I'm going in first,' he said. 'Just in case our friendly neighbourhood gravedigger got it wrong, and Mixer's still home. The rest of you can wait here until I give the all-clear.'

They watched as the investigator walked over to the door and gripped the brass door handle. There was a brief pause, and then he disappeared inside. Seconds later he came flying backwards out of one of the ground-floor windows. He had a gnome on top of him.

Flicka and Modeset rolled their eyes in sync.

The battle landed on the cobbles. After taking a few minor blows, Obegarde threw the gnome into a pile of rubbish bins and followed up his offensive with a well-aimed boot.

'I hate this guy,' he said, panting, as he pulled the unconscious gnome on to his feet. 'I absolutely, unutterably, one hundred per cent hate him. Jimmy, can you give me a hand getting him to the militia? He's got a nasty habit of giving me the slip.'

Jimmy nodded, and hurried over to help.

'We'll meet you at the palace in one hour, get this mess sorted out,' Obegarde called.

Modeset made to enter the hovel, then stopped and put a hand on Flicka's shoulder.

'You stay here and watch for the militia,' he commanded. 'We've got until Obegarde gets to the guardhouse to search the place; after that, it'll be crawling with the district's finest.'

Twenty-Five

The air in the hovel was musty.

'I'm up here,' called Flicka, from the top of the staircase. She'd abandoned her sentry post at the front door for a preferred position in the attic. It still afforded a fine view of the road, and she could search at the same time.

'OK,' Modeset shouted back. 'Tell me if you find anything.'

'Sure.'

'Right.'

Modeset stepped through a low door and looked around with unconcealed distaste at the room beyond.

The kitchen, like the rest of the hovel, was a threadbare affair. Rats congregated in the corner of the room and Modeset was sure he could see a vole into the bargain.

The only decent piece of furniture in the room, as far as he could tell, was an ageing iron stove that looked as though it might have value as scrap metal. It looked a little out of place, and, Modeset was sure, a little out of sync with the wall. He stepped over to the dresser, hunkered down, leant a shoulder against it, and, after several attempts, moved it aside. The wall behind sported several deep cracks. Modeset saw something wedged in the largest of these, and reached inside to pull it out. When he finally managed to wrench the obstacle free, he discovered it was in fact a book, and it weighed a ton.

He struggled over to the table and dropped the volume down with a spine-juddering smack.

'What was that?' shouted Flicka.

Modeset sighed.

'I've found a book,' he bellowed back.

Groaning with effort, he heaved the book over and allowed it to slam down. On the cover etched in golden letters, were the words;

E A   I   G
L E   N   S

Modeset squinted at the missing outlines of letters, blinked and looked again, but he still couldn't make any sense of the title. The he rubbed the palm of his hand over the gold lettering and, losing patience, brushed a mountain of dust from the cover. Thus revealed, the writing read:

LEAVING
LEGENDS

Modeset frowned.

'*Leaving Legends?*' he said aloud.

'What's that?' asked Flicka. She emerged from the doorway and slumped down, out of breath, on a crooked stool beside the table.

'It's one of the Yowler holy books, or some close approximation. As I recall, they were always dropping leaflets into the guild; some rot about paying weekly for a copy if your earnings can't make the stretch.'

'Except that this can't be a copy,' Flicka commented, nodding at the tome. 'I mean, look at it. It's got to be an original with all that braiding. I bet it was stolen. Nobody who lives *here* could afford a book like *that*.'

'Hmm ... as a matter of fact, it was stolen. From Karuim's Church, though by all accounts the theft was arranged.'

Flicka scratched at a cut on her chin.

'How do you know that?' she asked. 'Obegarde?'

'Yes. He paid them a visit last night. Whatever this whole, twisted mess is all about, I'll make a fair bet it has more than a little to do with this book.'

'You could be right, Lord M. What does it say?'

'I don't know. I'm not reading it here, that's for sure.'

Modeset tried to pick up the book, but it was clearly too heavy to carry halfway across the city. Only the gods knew how a *gnome* had managed it.

He sighed, opened the top leaf and began to read. After a few minutes, he looked up.

Flicka was staring expectantly at him.

'What does it say?' she hazarded.

Modeset shrugged.

'It's the usual religious drivel; starts off with some crazy prophet who's decided to resurrect Yowler, God of Scones-er-that might be Stones, I think. Yes, it is. Right, *anyway*, he tries to bring Yowler back to life by turning an entire town to stone.'

'How?'

Modeset continued to turn the pages.

'Erm . . . well, apparently, he took six special lizards called Batchtiki, and he put them into some kind of magic machine. There's a drawing of it here.' He thought back to the hulking monstrosity in the shadows of Warehouse Six, but the illustration looked nothing like it.

'It's totally different,' he muttered. 'Totally. There's not one similarity in the design.'

'I don't understand,' Flicka said, watching the duke as if lip-reading his thoughts. 'What are you talking about?'

Modeset pointed at the tome.

'Obegarde found and destroyed a gigantic machine in

one of the warehouses down at the harbour. It definitely had something to do with the Yowlers because the church was logged as the receiver. I saw it with my own eyes, but it bore absolutely no resemblance to this thing in here.' He jabbed a finger at the illustration. '*This* looks more like a lighthouse.'

'That's because it *is* a lighthouse,' Flicka ventured, peering over his shoulder. 'If you look closely there's an arrow next to the word "machine". You're on the wrong page.'

The duke reached down and turned over a leaf. On the new page was a picture that Modeset recognized immediately.

'That was it!' he exclaimed. 'That was the thing in the warehouse!' His gaze fell to the writing beneath it.

'The lighthouse,' Modeset continued, 'having been powered by the glare of a Batchtiki-holding device, fired a charge of energy into the target – our machine at the warehouse – freezing everything within a five-dinat radius.'

'What's a dinat?'

'Uh . . . about twenty miles,' Modeset guessed.

Flicka looked suddenly aghast.

'Th-they were going to turn the whole of Illmoor to stone!' she cried. 'Those crazy, cretinous murderers! If Obegarde hadn't destroyed the machine—'

Modeset clicked his fingers for silence.

'So,' he began, brows knotting with the effort of

deduction, 'if it was the receptacle in the warehouse, and we can now reasonably assume that this was the case, then we no longer have that portion of the problem to worry about.'

'There's a but coming, isn't there?'

'I'm afraid so,' Modeset warned. 'Because it also says that the secondary machine is used to magnify the beam's resulting discharge. So one machine fires into the other, which magnifies the beam and explodes. Now, even allowing for the destruction of its magnifier, we can comfortably assume that the remaining beam's strike would still take in all of Dullitch and a little more besides.'

'B-b-but that means we're all going to get tur—'

'All it means, *Flicka*, is that we need to find the primary machine. Pronto.'

As the girl's smile froze, the duke read on, turning pages with increasing fervour.

'Ha! Here is where it gets interesting,' he said. ' "Distance and Trajectories": according to Doiley's first law, the machines have to be at least seventy miles apart.'

'That's an incredible distance,' said Flicka, who'd excelled in geography during a brief stint with the Cartography School. 'Especially since the whole of Illmoor is only eighty miles, north to south.'

'OK,' said Modeset, eyeing her carefully. 'For the sake of argument, let's say that's right. You're good at geography, yes?'

'Yes,' Flicka replied confidently. 'So?'

'Well, what's at the other end of the continent?'

'Sorry?'

'Well, Dullitch occupies the southernmost point of eastern Illmoor, right?'

'Right.'

'So, is there a town in the extreme north, past Grinswood?'

Flicka's face creased as she tried to recall the outline of the big wall-mounted map in the Chief Cartographer's office, but it was Modeset who answered his own question.

'PLUNGE!' he exclaimed. 'Plunge is the northernmost town on the continent. Arrrgh!'

Flicka nearly jumped out of her skin. She gawped at the duke, who suddenly looked as if he was about to kill someone.

'What's wrong?' she said, dubiously.

'Plunge falls within the jurisdiction of Fogrise,' snapped Modeset. 'My land!'

'Well, not technically *yours*, Lord M,' Flicka pointed out. 'At least not any more: those old boundaries haven't existed for years! Besides, it's *miles* away from Fogrise.'

'Yes, but it's still *my* land, my birthright, and it's like they're firing a deadly beam from my back garden to destroy Dullitch! It's the principle of the thing! I'd feel responsible!' Modeset let out a long, depressed sigh. 'What am I going to do?'

'Stop them turning us all to stone?' Flicka hazarded. 'It's just an idea, but— What? What did I say?'

Suddenly a light flickered in the duke's eyes, as if he'd been sitting in a corner for years and someone had just remembered to plug him in. Destiny beckoned. It told Modeset, in the confines of his head, that the time had come to take a stand, to do something truly heroic.

'C'mon, Flicka,' he snapped. 'We're going to avert a catastrophe. Your first, my second.'

'OK, Lord M. What're we going to do?'

'Well, *I'm* going to begin by reading this book from cover to cover and then we're going back to the Steeplejack to fetch my battle attire. After that, I need to speak with my cousin.'

'Are we going to get Pegrand?'

'Yes, among other things; now keep a watch for those guards while I catch up on some history!'

Twenty-Six

Viscount Curfew was surprised to see his cousin march into the palace throne room wearing a full suit of Fogrise armour. To increase the level of bewilderment (made evident by the shocked gasps of the royal bodyguards lurking in the shadows of the room), Modeset saluted.

'Apologies for the disturbance, my lord,' he said. 'But Dullitch is in grave danger, and I feel I owe it to the city to warn you.'

Curfew licked his lips. For some reason the duke's renewed strength of voice was concerning him.

'Um . . . grave danger, you say? Any chance you could be a little more specific?'

'A plot is underway . . .'

'Yes, I'm quite awa—'

'. . . to resurrect a dark god.'

Curfew paused, lowered his hand. 'Oh' was all he could manage.

'This resurrection,' Modeset continued, 'may involve the people of Dullitch being turned to stone.'

Curfew swallowed a few times, and steepled his fingers.

'You have proof of this, I assume?' he said unsteadily. 'Such accusations are fruitless without—'

'Eyewitnesses can be provided later. Right now my needs are great. If I'm to stop this plot I will require a mage of some considerable skill to teleport a small company to Plunge.'

A look of sudden, terrible recognition settled on the viscount's face.

'Plunge,' he said slowly. 'Of course.'

'Well, do you have a mage or don't you?'

'Yes, I mean no! Absolutely not! Magic is outlawed in Dullitch, as you are well aware. I can, however, provide you with—'

'Horses simply won't make the journey in time and I don't know anyone with a dragon.'

Curfew got to his feet, straightened up.

'I'm not supplying you with magic unless I'm absolutely one hundred per cent satisfied that a definite threat is posed to the city.'

'Very well,' Modeset agreed, leaning across the viscount's marble desk and staring him directly in the eye. 'A beam comprised of the glare of several Batchtiki lizards is to be fired from a small machine through a sorcery-fuelled lighthouse lens into the sun. The resulting beam *was* going to hit a specially constructed magnifier in Dullitch. Now, as I understand, the receptacle has been destroyed—'

'Yes, entirely.'

'But that does not discount the fact that a beam will be fired and, though the resulting range will undoubtedly be reduced, I feel certain the malevolent group involved will inflict many, many deaths with it. Satisfied?'

Before Curfew could question him further, the duke stepped forward and placed both hands flat on the desktop.

'Now,' he began, eyeing the bodyguards who had begun to creep from the shadows. 'Do you have a mage in the building or not?'

The viscount held up a hand.

'Yes . . . very well.'

The guards receded.

'I do hope you know what you're doing, Cousin,' Curfew warned.

Modeset took a step back, saluted again.

'How many men are you taking with you?' the viscount prompted.

'Three, my lord,' said Modeset confidently. 'And one woman.'

Twenty-Seven

Many miles away from the palace, in a great lighthouse atop the tiny town of Plunge, the Lark paced back and forth before a wide window that looked out upon the sea.

'Well,' she said, not bothering to turn when she heard the door creak open. 'Was our little experiment a success?'

'Yes, Mistress,' said Moors, trying to control his excitement with a nervous laugh. 'But I'm afraid Edwy got a little carried away.'

'Oh?' The Lark twirled around, her robed arms folded in annoyance. 'Do explain.'

Moors hauled himself further into the room, practically blocking out all light from the passage behind him.

'Well, I *changed* the villagers exactly as you said, Mistress: slowly, one at a time. But Edwy started trying to do two at once, then three and four, and—'

'I get the picture,' the Lark snapped. 'So we now have the entire town under wraps, do we?'

Moors managed a sheepish nod.

'I'm afraid so, Mistress. I did *warn* him not to go too far, but you know Edwy, Mistress, he doesn't listen.'

The Lark shook her head.

'No,' she echoed, quietly. 'He'll pay for that. Still, no matter, the test can be considered a success.'

'Yes, Mistress,' Moors bleated. 'Is there anything else we should be doing?'

The Lark nodded quickly.

'There is. Fetch Edwy; we're going to accelerate our plans a little. Dullitch falls tonight!'

Twenty-Eight

The cellar beneath Dullitch Palace was in an absolute uproar.

'Are you sure this man's playing with a full deck?' Modeset demanded, pointing across the room at the viscount's resident (and highly classified) sorcerer.

It was no wonder Curfew kept Wrickshaw Muldoon in the basement. The old man had a face like the first actor in a play to forget his lines. He was impossibly ancient, excruciatingly wizened and uncomfortably short-sighted.

'You,' he announced, suddenly thrusting out an arm. 'Do not dare speak ill of my powers.'

Modeset rolled his eyes.

'I'm over this way,' he said.

'I knew THAT! I was just testing your reflexes.'

'Ha! Are any of you listening to this rubbish? We'd have more luck being teleported by an incontinent whippet.'

'Can we please get on?' said Curfew, holding up a hand for silence. 'Good. Now, can everyone intent on saving our city please step into the circle of voluntary transportation?'

There was a lot of mumbling, and several city dignitaries secreted themselves in remote corners of the cellar. Modeset remained, accompanied by Flicka and Pegrand Marshall, his newly released manservant. Obegarde also occupied the inside of the circle, stepping aside to admit the reluctant figure of Jimmy Quickstint.

'Why am I doing this again?' the gravedigger asked, muttering under his breath when nobody provided an answer.

'Very good,' Curfew applauded. 'Now, are you all ready to go to Plunge?'

'Yes.'

'Yeah.'

'S'pose so.'

'Do we have any choice?'

Curfew beamed.

'Superb! Now, if you would be so kind, Mr Muldoon?'

The sorcerer stepped forward, raised one withered arm and promptly turned one of the skulking officials into a herring.

The group, as one, swallowed. Modeset looked daggers at the old man.

'Does he have any idea what he's doing?'

'Please control your temper, Cousin. I'm sure Mr

Muldoon was merely warming up, isn't that right, Wrickshaw?'

Muldoon nodded, gave a lop-sided smile and began to concentrate again. A few moments later, Modeset disappeared in a puff of smoke. Flicka coughed and spluttered in the resulting cloud, and Obegarde had to thrust out an arm in order to block Jimmy's sudden bid for escape.

Pegrand gasped, and stumbled in bewildered awe towards the place where Modeset had been standing. He hadn't quite reached the spot when he too winked out of existence. Flicka was the third to evaporate, but then a lengthy pause ensued.

'What's the problem?' Obegarde bellowed. Jimmy looked faintly hopeful.

Curfew strode over to the old sorcerer and leaned in close; whispers were exchanged.

'There is no problem, I assure you,' said the viscount calmly. 'Mr Muldoon simply requires a few moments in which to regain his energy.'

The loftwing sighed. 'Can't he just get on with it?'
Curfew swallowed.

'Mr Obegarde, you must understand that if our sorcerer is not able to recuperate his powers, he might not be able to send you to Plunge in one piece.'

'We don't have time,' Obegarde said. 'I'll take the risk.'

'Fantastic,' Jimmy mumbled. 'I bet I lose all my favourite bits.'

Part Three

The Fight for Plunge

One

Plunge Bay stood on the northern fringe of Illmoor, at a point where the Grinswood gave way to the Mountains of Mavokhan. In the past, it *had* been a picturesque little town full of fat, friendly fishermen and their bloated, odious wives. It *had* been a place where the aristocrats of Dullitch sent their children during the height of summer, and a place where retired wizards came to settle down and raise magically inept sons and dizzy daughters who always got into the kind of trouble a wand couldn't fix.

Plunge Bay *had* been all these things and more besides. Now, however, it was . . .

'Empty, milord; the town's a complete morgue.'

Pegrand Marshall, standing in the middle of the street with his blunderbuss at the ready, squinted up to the roof of the nearest house to try and determine whether Duke

Modeset had heard him. Flicka was still materializing at the far end of the street. Jimmy Quickstint and Obegarde were, as yet, nowhere to be seen.

'It's EMPTY!' he bellowed again, just in case.

'I heard you the first time, Pegrand,' said a voice beside him.

Modeset shimmered into view, his form becoming a little less hazy as the materialization spell wore off. Evidently, his own journey through enchantment had been a little less smooth than that of his companions.

'I don't like it,' he said. 'It's not right. A whole town can't just disappear. Have a look inside some of those houses, will you?'

The manservant hurried over to one of the doors and hammered on it using its ornamental brass knocker. When he got no reply, he slipped inside and reappeared minutes later sporting a worried grin.

'There is a woman in there, milord,' he said. 'But she's been turned to stone.'

Pegrand tried rapping on another door further down the street. To his surprise, Obegarde answered it.

'Found the loftwing, milord! He came down in the butcher's . . .'

Thunder rumbled off to the east, a distant echo of sound. Somehow, it made the vacancy of Plunge seem even more forbidding; doors creaked open in the wind and dust gathered on neglected panes.

Flicka rushed up to join the duke, still fiddling with

her clothes in a distracted manner; she felt sure that the spell had distorted the fabric. Obegarde looked even worse; the investigator kept shaking his head and had apparently lost the power of speech into the bargain.

Pegrand hunched his shoulders and rubbed his wrists.

'What're we dealing with here, milord?' he asked, beginning to stare off into the distance.

'A difficult prospect,' Modeset answered. 'But at least we know we're in the right place. Presumably, the unfortunate population of Plunge have been exposed to the glare of the lizards as some sort of preparative experiment for the turning to stone of Dullitch.'

'We need some sort of weapon,' Obegarde piped up, peering around the empty streets. 'Something bigger than that blunderbuss: a siege cannon, maybe. Something major . . .'

They watched as he disappeared down a side alley, only to re-emerge from the mouth of a second, some distance along the road. He beckoned to them, then suddenly veered left.

'Where's he off to?' said Modeset, nudging Pegrand in the ribs to shake the manservant from his reverie.

'Dunno, milord. I'll try and get his attention.' Pegrand flung up his arms and started shouting.

'Will you shut up, Pegrand! You'll alert the Yowlers! We'll catch him up, OK?'

'Right, milord. Sorry.'

'Hmm . . . I'm hearing that a lot from you, lately. You

haven't been yourself since we shared the dog kennel. Did you hit your head or something?'

'I don't remember, milord. I ate a few funny-shaped biscuits, but—'

'Never mind. Where's young Jimmy got to?'

'Don't think he's arrived yet, milord. Flicka's disappeared as well.'

'Oh, for goodness' sake; where is everybody? We've only been here five minutes and we're already a total shambles!'

'Quiet, milord! You'll alert the Yowlers.'

Modeset cast a sharp glance at Pegrand, then clipped him round the ear.

two

'Sorry, Lord M,' Flicka said, when the duke and Pegrand had caught up with her on the first floor of one of the fishermen's cottages. 'But I had to get a closer look at the peninsula and I just knew one of these rooms would overlook the bay. I haven't seen Jimmy yet. I hope the spell didn't go wrong or anything . . .'

Pegrand shrugged and began to rummage through the cupboards.

'No weapons here,' he said eventually, and ripped one of the doors off for good measure. 'Have to rely on me and my blunderbuss, milord.'

'May the gods have mercy,' said Obegarde conquering the stairs of the cottage and leaning half-heartedly against the door frame.

'Find anything?'

'No,' said the loftwing, sulkily. 'Not so much as a knuckleduster.'

'Great. You all right, milord?'

Modeset, still taken aback by the stone statue of a small boy beside the window, didn't reply. He took a moment to mentally rewind what Flicka had said earlier.

'What peninsula?' he said to her, when he'd finished his thinking process.

'The one with the lighthouse on the end,' said Flicka, gesturing out of the window towards a towering column just visible in the distance. 'I noticed it from the end of the road, while you were talking. There's a localized storm there, which is odd. It's a little *too* localized if you ask me.'

'*Sorcery*,' said Modeset, eyes narrowing. 'Our friends from the church, no doubt.'

Pegrand marched over to the window and squinted out.

'Should we go in guns blazing, milord?' he asked.

'No thank you, Pegrand. That will not be necessary until after you've learned how to operate the weapon you're carrying.'

The manservant frowned.

'How do you mean, milord?'

'Well, for starters, the barrel is pointing *towards* your chest . . .'

Pegrand glanced down.

'Oh, will you look at that? So it is.'

'. . . meaning that if you'd heard a noise on the way up here and had, in reacting, pulled the trigger, Flicka and I would now be scraping sections of your ribcage from the walls.'

'Point taken, milord.'

'Jolly good. Now, I want you to hand the blunderbuss over to Obegarde.'

'Oh, do I have to?'

'Immediately and without argument.'

'But, why?'

'Because, dear friend, I have to focus my mind on defeating the enemies of Dullitch, and I'm going to find that extremely difficult if I have to keep looking over my shoulder in case you accidentally blow my head off with your six seconds' ballistic experience. OK?'

Pegrand mumbled something under his breath, and shoved the gun towards Obegarde, who accepted it with no particular show of emotion.

'Now,' Modeset continued. 'We're going to make for the lighthouse.'

'I don't fancy walking into the jaws of death without good reason, milord,' said Pegrand. 'Something'll have us a cropper, I'm telling you.'

The duke sighed.

'I don't have time to argue,' he said, pleasantly. 'Suffice to say, old friend, that if I'm going, then so are you.'

Three

Modeset and company were on their way over to the lighthouse when Pegrand suddenly barked an announcement.

'The sabre! The silver sabre!'

Modeset and Flicka froze; Obegarde took a deep breath.

'What?' the duke asked, bewildered.

'The sacred silver sabre.'

'What ARE you talking about?'

'The sacred silver sabre of Bowlcock, milord!'

Modeset frowned at his manservant.

'Bowlcock,' he said, slowly. 'You mean—'

'The first duke of Dullitch,' Pegrand confirmed, with a sudden grin. 'The greatest warrior who ever walked the land. On his deathbed, he donated his sacred silver sabre, the weapon that'd never failed him, to a museum in Plunge! It must still be here somewhere!'

'How do you know all that?' asked Modeset, aghast at the possibility that the final movements of his greatest ancestor had escaped him.

Pegrand looked nonplussed.

'I read it in the *Collected Histories of Dullitch*, milord. Volume Six, I believe. If we can find the museum, we'll find the sabre.'

'I don't understand,' Flicka chimed in. 'Why would we want it?'

Pegrand gasped.

'Why would we want it? The sacred silver sabre of Bowlcock? We'd *want* it because it's a charmed weapon. Bowlcock never lost a single fight with it. He took on dragons, wyverns, trolls, giants and an army of greenskins. It's got . . .'

'. . . historical significance,' Modeset finished. 'Yes, I can appreciate that. Destiny has its wily ways. Besides, in a town this size, it shouldn't take too long to find the museum.'

Obegarde made a sucking sound with his cheeks.

'I'll wait here,' he said, 'but do remember that lives may well be at stake. We haven't got all day!'

Four

Three and a half hours of frantic searching had laid bare the Plunge treasury, gold reserve, bakery, butchers, merchants' tenement, armoury, food stores and blacksmiths' forge; not to mention fourteen private houses.

All the while Obegarde stood in the town square, tapping his foot and kicking the occasional wall.

'I don't believe this,' said Pegrand, sighing and stamping his foot on the dusty floor of yet another food store. 'They must eat like rabid animals.'

'It's a pity we haven't got a map of some kind,' said Modeset.

'There's a place we've missed.'

'Yes, a map!' Pegrand agreed, ignoring the brief interruption. 'There would have to be one in the town hall.'

'Town hall's full of statues,' said Modeset, dismissively. 'There must've been a big meeting or something. I assume the villagers were all caught unawares; it's like Medusa's garden, in there.'

Modeset frowned suddenly.

'What do you mean, "a place we missed"?' he demanded, turning to Flicka. She was standing with her arms folded, gazing nonchalantly out to sea.

'Well?' Modeset prompted. 'What place?'

'A big building with brass dogs outside, right next to the town gates. We've walked past it five times; I *have* been trying to tell you but nobody seemed to be listening.'

'Very well,' said Modeset, stung by the tiny flicker of embarrassment he always felt whenever he looked directly at her. 'We'll check it out at once, but I'd prefer it if we take the back alley; I don't think I could bear walking past Obegarde after his last outburst.'

The door to Plunge Museum was locked. Modeset eventually had to break a window in order to gain entrance.

Inside, the building was dark and shadowy. Glass display cases crowded the walls and a heavy candelabrum hung down from a grand mosaic ceiling.

'I'll start on the left,' said Modeset. The others mumbled in agreement and wandered off towards various cases huddled in bleak corners of the room.

The first case, Modeset noted with no great interest,

contained the skull of Baron Huckstep, a little-known retainer of the Plunge crest, who helped rescue the town from a great dragon back in the Dual Age. It was in two separate pieces.

Next up, after the vertebrae of several infamous (and rather less than respectable) marquesses, came the legendary Tarnish Helmet which had almost saved Sir Cuffock from the Witches of Rinstare. Judging by the shape of it – an inverted L – the margin of survival had been pretty narrow (evidently, unlucky for some).

Modeset sighed. He found himself wondering what the people of Dullitch would keep as a reminder of *him*. A nose hair, perhaps, or some earwax? No, he reflected, it would probably be something like 'the gold tooth of Duke Modeset' with a footnote declaring 'the only thing of any value we found on him'. He scowled at the thought, and moved on.

He was studying a metal clasp belonging to some long-forgotten king when a gasp from Pegrand disturbed his concentration.

'What is it, man?' he called over.

'It's this bloke, here. They've only got his whatsit on a plinth!'

The duke sighed.

'I don't want to know, Pegrand,' he said, flatly.

'His whatsit, though, milord! His actual *whatsit*.'

'Yes, so you said.'

'He must've been pretty successful with the women for 'em to want to remember him like that.'

'Yes, I'm sure. Now please forget about it and continue your search.' He turned to look behind him. 'Any luck yet, Flicka?'

The aide shook her head, and mumbled negatively.

Modeset returned his attention to the line of cases he'd been perusing. Then he stopped short.

'Pegrand,' he said slowly. 'You told us about Lord Bowlcock's generous donation of the sacred silver sabre to Plunge Museum, do you remember?'

The manservant was quick to frown.

'Of course I do, milord,' he said.

Modeset swallowed and tried to hide the unease in his voice.

'Well, would you like to know what *else* the great lord donated to the museum?'

'Um . . . yes. What?'

'Himself.'

'Sorry, milord?'

'Lord Bowlcock,' Modeset repeated, pronouncing each word with extreme care, 'donated himself, along with the super sabre you were talking about.'

'It's there? The sabre's actually there?'

'Oh, yes. In fact, he's still holding it. Only he doesn't look all that keen to let it go.'

Pegrand hurried over, Flicka trailing behind him.

The skeleton beyond the glass barrier was still

clutching the silver sabre with both hands. It looked ancient in the true sense of the word, not merely long decrepit but well and truly worm-ridden; so off the coil as to be almost non-existent.

Pegrand reach out to touch the glass, but Modeset stayed his hand.

'Wait, man! What if it's cursed?'

'Cursed, milord? What, Lord Bowlcock or the sword?'

'Both!'

'Well of course it's up to you, milord,' said the manservant, stepping back. 'But look at the luck we've had so far.'

Modeset nodded.

'Good point,' he said. 'I'll grab it, then, if you don't mind.'

'Of course not, milord.'

Pegrand and Flicka stood back as the duke looked around for something to throw at the case. Eventually, he settled on an old wooden stool behind the entrance doors.

The glass shattered.

'Right,' Modeset announced. 'Here goes nothing.'

Mindful of the glass shards, he leaned into the display case and began the difficult task of removing Lord Bowlcock's clasped fingers from the silver sabre.

'I'd have thought that they'd just crumble away, milord,' said Pegrand helpfully.

'Hmm . . . it seems not.' In less than a minute, Modeset

had resorted to applying pressure on the upper arm with his boot. 'I certainly didn't expect this much resistance.'

He gave one final wrench and staggered back, clutching not only the silver sabre but Lord Bowlcock's arm as well.

'Damnation! Of all the luck!'

'Hold on, milord. I'll help you out, there.'

Pegrand and Modeset played tug-of-war with the sword arm and sabre for what seemed like an age.

'Flicka!' snapped the duke. 'Get over here and help us, will you?'

Flicka joined in, but to no avail.

'Very well,' Modeset said, face flushed with a mixture of embarrassment and fury. 'We'll leave the arm on; I'll use the sabre as it is.'

'You can't do that, Lord M,' Flicka warned. 'You'll do yourself an injury.'

'She's right there, milord,' added Pegrand. 'Every time you swing it round the elbow'll catch you on the chin. It'll be like fighting two opponents at once.'

Modeset raised the sabre and, ignoring the arm that dangled down from it, smiled proudly.

'Pegrand,' he began. 'This is my ancestor, my flesh and blood. He will not impede my victory!'

He took an experimental swing with the sword and yelped when its appendage almost took off his ear.

Obegarde, arriving at the museum just in time to witness the display, clicked his tongue and sighed deeply.

'When you've all quite finished running around this cement garden of a town, raiding food stores and perusing museums, do you think that there's even the slightest smidgeon of a chance that you might accompany me to the lighthouse in an attempt to save the entire population of a certain city? You know, if it's not too much trouble?' He made to leave, then turned and strode up to Flicka, depositing the blunderbuss in her hands.

'You take this,' he commanded. 'I'm better off fighting the old-fashioned way.'

Five

'They're coming, Mistress, they're coming!'

Edwy burst through the door to the top floor of the lighthouse, his breath almost failing him as he hurtled to a halt.

The Lark was preoccupied with her glare machine.

'Mmm . . . who is?' she said, distractedly.

'City folk, Mistress! There's a group of them.'

The Lark released her grip on the machine and spun around, her attention suddenly seized.

'Inconceivable! Who are they?'

'One of them is the man I saw in Dullitch; he came to the temple to speak with Lopsalm.'

'The wretched loftwing. Hmm . . . that would make sense. I thought I felt an invasive little mind trying to read my thoughts. Still, he got here exceptionally fast, which is concerning . . .'

'Yes, Mistress. Mixer failed you, Mistress.'

'Of course he did; I'm surrounded by incompetents. What about the other members of this raiding party? Who are they?'

'I don't know, Mistress; I can't quite make them out. What should we do?'

'Nothing. You've done enough already.'

Edwy bowed his head.

'Yes, Mistress.'

'For now, I need you to take control of the machine. It's being primed, and the glare is being collected. Keep it aimed through the lighthouse lens, but do not release the beam until I return – that is MY birthright.'

Edwy bowed and took over at the reins of the machine.

'What are you going to do, Mistress?'

The Lark secured her hair in a ponytail, and smiled cruelly.

'I'm going to kill a vampire.'

She turned and swept out of the room, calling behind her, 'If Moors comes lumbering up here, tell him to guard the floor below.'

'Yes, Mistress. I will, Mistress.'

Six

The peninsula leading to Plunge Lighthouse was long and winding, and the approach offered much in the way of conveniently placed bushes. Modeset and company nipped from cover to cover as they neared the towering structure.

The storm that had been hovering over the lighthouse had diminished considerably, but an ethereal glow still warned of magical activity inside.

Modeset dashed straight to the door, giving an indication to Pegrand who joined him to kick at the door. Unfortunately, all they got was a dull thud. Even Obegarde's hardened boot couldn't penetrate the door.

'Flicka,' Modeset said, turning abruptly on his heel. 'The door, if you please.'

Flicka nodded, looked along the barrel of the blunderbuss, and pulled the trigger.

Nothing happened.

'She's not doing it right,' Pegrand said, snatching the weapon and re-aiming it. *He* pulled the trigger.

Nothing happened.

'Let me see that,' Flicka snapped, yanking the weapon back. She turned it over a few times, and sighed. 'You can't fire it because it's not real,' she said.

'Eh?'

'What do you mean?'

She shrugged.

'It's only the *model* of a blunderbuss. Where did you say you got it from?'

'That elf guard gave it to me,' the manservant muttered, looking down at his feet. 'You know, the one who his lordship assaulted—'

'Fantastic, Pegrand, and you didn't think this generous gift was a little odd?'

Modeset straightened up.

'Right,' he said, speaking with renewed authority. 'I'm going to climb up to one of the lower windows and break through. Then I'll crawl inside, disarm the guards (assuming there are guards), run down and let you both in. I'll need help getting up, though. Perhaps we can form a sort of human ladder . . .'

Pegrand and Flicka both looked extremely doubtful.

'This is a joke,' Obegarde warned. 'I'll have no part of it.'

'Please yourself.'

'Oh, come *on*. There must be another way.'

'As I said, Obegarde, please *yourself*. You're your own man.'

Modeset disappeared around the base of the lighthouse. A few seconds later, he returned.

'It's far too high,' he said. 'Pegrand, you get do—'

He was interrupted by a small clap of lightning and a sudden puff of smoke. Jimmy Quickstint winked into existence, hovered in mid-air for a few seconds and then collapsed on to the ground beside the lighthouse.

'Where did you come from?' Pegrand demanded. 'More to the point, where in the name of Urgumflux the Wormridden did you *go*?'

A strangely tortured smile appeared on the gravedigger's gormless face. 'I think I got a bit stretched,' he announced in a far-off voice. 'In fact, it feels like only a bit of me is here.'

'Yes,' Flicka chirped. 'You're right about that. In fact, if I were you I should go down to the village right now and find some clothes to put on.'

Jimmy looked down, and gulped.

Seven

'Pegrand, keep still down there!'

'Hold on, milord! I'm trying to get Flicka's foot off my shoulder.'

'Don't do that, man! We'll all collapse!'

'But she's digging it in on purpose, milord!'

'I *am* not. It's Jimmy, he's buckling!'

'Well, what do you expect? This apron doesn't fit me! Besides, Obegarde keeps tickling my feet!'

Modeset stood at the top of the human tower, fingernails scratching for purchase on the pasty surface of the lighthouse wall. He was about an inch short of the ledge at the base of the lowest window.

'Pegrand, stand on tiptoe!'

'Arrgghhh!'

The tower was raised a little, and Modeset's searching

fingers found the ledge. He scrambled up and rolled
inside the window. Behind him, the tower collapsed.
Pegrand folded up and Flicka managed to roll but Jimmy
landed awkwardly and knocked himself unconscious.
Obegarde shook his head sadly.

'Well you can count the boy out. Look at him – he's
stone cold!'

Flicka moved to kneel beside the gravedigger (who'd
managed to acquire a baker's apron from one of the houses
nearest the lighthouse), cradling his head in her arms.

'Are you OK, Jimmy? Can you hear me?'

'He's all right,' said Pegrand. 'He's still breathing, you
see?'

Flicka forced a weak smile.

'He's been through a lot,' she said. 'Maybe we should
leave him be. You lot go on, I'll stay here with him, make
sure he's all right.'

The manservant nodded.

'See you around, then,' he said.

'Good luck,' said Flicka. 'Don't get turned to stone or
anything.'

'Yeah, right. We'll try not to.'

Pegrand took one last look at the pale face of Jimmy
Quickstint and made for the lighthouse door.

'Hello?'

Pegrand peered around the door of the lighthouse,
swallowed and stepped inside.

'Are you up there, milord?' he said, moving aside as Obegarde stepped across the threshold.

'No, I'm behind the door,' said Modeset.

'Oh, I am sorry, Sir. I thought you'd be at the top by now.'

Modeset smiled humourlessly. Then he wrestled himself free from the gap between the wall and the door, and staggered to the foot of the stairs. The lighthouse was engulfed in a thick, forced silence; the kind that usually precedes an explosion. However, before Modeset could remark on this, a resounding click signalled the closing of a door at least three floors above them.

He glanced sideways at Pegrand and, finding no encouraging smile from that quarter, took a reluctant step forward and prepared to mount the spiral staircase.

'Well, here goes,' he said. The manservant nodded in a way that indicated he'd be bringing up the rear from somewhere near Dullitch.

'I'm not sure if we should be doing this, milord,' whispered Pegrand. 'I mean, this Lark's one of them magical types, right? So this is a job for a wizard, surely.'

'In any other town, yes. But Plunge falls within the jurisdiction of Fogrise Keep and, therefore, it's a job for me.'

'But you don't even like the place, milord.'

'What has fondness got to do with it? Fogrise towns are my towns, by inheritance. It's the principle of the thing.'

'I suppose so. But, by that argument, what about the time when Wild Chives attacked Brimtown?'

Modeset sighed.

'What about it?'

'You said the villagers could all burn.'

Obegarde sniggered.

'Nonsense,' Modeset snapped. 'I would never encourage vandalism in the Fogrise communities.'

'Eh? You gave 'em the money for torches, didn't you? And that siege cannon of theirs had "sponsored by Modeset" along the side.'

'Yes, well, those were very hard times, Pegrand. Back then we sold out to oppression. Now we're fighting for, for—'

'A sack of lizards,' Obegarde interrupted. 'Essentially.'

'Well, yes, *essentially*.' The duke took a moment to consider things. 'Hardly seems worth all the effort, does it?'

The investigator shrugged.

'Not sure; I've never gone much on morality. I suppose one way of looking at it would be to say that we're trying to save an endangered species as well as a city. That's assuming everything Jimmy told us about the bird is true.'

'Yes, you're absolutely right! Onward and upward, as they say.'

Modeset drew the sacred silver sabre and hurried up the stairs, trying to keep Lord Bowlcock's flaccid arm tucked under his own. Pegrand waited until he was out of sight and then followed sheepishly after him, but Obegarde remained rooted to the spot. Something very interesting had caught his attention.

Eight

There were two doors on the first landing of the lighthouse. Sabre drawn (literally) at arm's length, Modeset stood on the landing, glancing nervously from one to the other. Eventually Pegrand padded up the last few stairs and almost collapsed. He leaned against the wall for support while he got his breath back.

'Oh, for goodness' sake, man,' Modeset whispered. 'When was the last time you took some exercise?'

Pegrand shrugged.

'Dunno, milord,' he managed. 'I can't remember much before my eighth birthday.'

'You mean you haven't taken any kind of exercise since you were eight?'

'Well . . .'

'Do you know how dangerous that is?'

'Not sure, milord. About as dangerous as tryin' to stop a mad priestess from turnin' a city to stone?'

'Yes, very amusing, Pegrand. We'll have to look into your fitness.'

'If we survive this, you mean?'

'Exactly. Now, are you going to take the left- or the right-hand door?'

The manservant shrugged.

'Er, well, seein' as you've got the sabre, milord, I thought I might just wait out here on the landing.'

'OK, in that case we'll go in together. The question remains; left or right?'

Pegrand took a good long stare at each option.

'I read somewhere that evil is always defined as the left-hand path, milord.'

'Right it is, then.'

'Hang about; isn't this woman we're after supposed to be evil?'

'Oh for goodness' sake, make your mind up, man! They'll have turned Dullitch to stone by the time we've put in an appearance!'

Modeset darted forward and put a shoulder to the left-hand door. When, after three or four charges, the door still hadn't given way, he turned the handle instead.

'Unlocked, milord! There's a turn-up for the books.'

Modeset gripped his shoulder in agony.

'I really hate you, Pegrand.'

'Ha! You're a fair old joker, milord.'

'Yes . . . now come on. Let's move.'

'Right behind you, milord.'

The manservant stepped aside to let his master in front, shivering with cold as Modeset used the edge of the sabre to urge open the door. It creaked back on tired hinges.

The room beyond was unremarkable in structure. With no doors, one minuscule barred window and no furniture to speak of, it felt like a prison cell. The only thing of any interest was the cage full of baby lizards nestling in the far corner.

Modeset's reaction was instinctive, if a little peculiar. He flung the arm 'n' sabre wide, dropped on to his stomach and buried his head in his hands.

'Look away, Pegrand!' he cried. 'It's them! It's the Batchtiki! Look away quickly!'

'Oh come on, milord. You don't honestly believe—'

Silence.

Modeset moaned, and hammered his fists on the floor. Then, expecting the worst, he raised his head, eyes tightly shut against the glares he could still feel harpooning him.

'Pegrand? Pegrand! Answer me now, man!'

Silence.

Modeset reached for his sword, grasped it by the arm and began to pull himself around to face the door. Eventually, he opened his eyes.

The manservant had been frozen in mid-step. His

mouth formed a surprised O and his eyes were glazed.

Modeset fought to control his temper; any sudden outburst would inevitably alert the machine-operator on the roof.

Remembering the folklore passages in *Leaving Legends*, Modeset used his shining silver wrist guard to view the Batchtiki. The reflection showed him that there were five of them in the cage, all of whom seemed impatient to escape.

Modeset got to his feet and, heaving Pegrand's statue behind him, hurried from the room and slammed the door shut. Outside on the landing, he propped the manservant against the east wall and made for the opposite room, which fortunately turned out to contain a small armoury.

Nine

The shape was so slight that at first Obegarde thought he was seeing things. It started as a small orb, spinning in one corner of the ceiling, just below the first flight of the spiral staircase. Neither Modeset nor Pegrand had noticed it, but Obegarde's superior vision had picked up the glimmer immediately. Now, somewhat worryingly considering their intended ambush, it was flashing red and green.

Obegarde cursed, and was about to hunt around outside for a suitable stone to throw at it when the globe suddenly began to grow. Descending as it swelled, the globe reformed into the sharp and extremely intimidating features of a woman. She was attractive, raven-haired and emanated a presence quite unlike any Obegarde had encountered before.

He tried to run, but his legs wouldn't move. He stood rooted to the spot as the facial image shimmered and expanded into an elfin figure, which emerged from the light-pool.

'Modeset!' Obegarde cried, fighting against his own inability to escape paralysis by the Lark. 'Pegrand! Jimmy! Flicka! Anybody! Help me out here!'

Somehow, the words became muffled as soon as they left his lips. He actually felt the sound reverberate and die before him. The reply, however, was not so impaired.

'The loftwing, I presume. Let us silence you first, shall we?'

The Lark stepped forward, mumbling unrepeatable syllables under her breath, and quite calmly closed a claw-like hand around his neck. She drove her other hand into his chest, and he felt fingernails like sharpened glass pierce his heart.

Obegarde threw punches and kicks that would have devastated a mountain troll, but still the Lark maintained her stranglehold, still she pierced his heart. He staggered backwards, feeling the life draining from his body. Finally, in a last-ditch attempt to fight his way out, he tightened his jaw muscles, extending fangs until they curved in a wide arc from both jaws. Then he ceased his backward drive and darted forward, biting sharply into the Lark's exposed neck.

'Ahhhhhh!'

She screamed and stumbled back, but in doing so she

closed her fist around the loftwing's heart. Clutching at the fresh wound in her neck, she yanked her arm from the vampire and fell against the wall.

Obegarde gave one last smile of satisfaction, and collapsed in a heap on the floor.

Still grasping the bite on her neck, the Lark pushed herself from the wall. She gave the loftwing an experimental prod with her foot. He was dead.

'Interesting that the city's resistance should include a vampire,' she said, as if the now silent Obegarde could still hear her. 'How ... quaint. Oh well, onward and upward.'

She folded her dark cloak about her and promptly vanished in a puff of smoke.

Ten

Armed with a short bow, two throwing daggers, Lord Bowlcock's arm and its trusty sabre, Modeset negotiated the rest of the spiral staircase and found himself in a small passage with a ladder leading to a trapdoor in the roof. A repulsively obese man stood on guard duty. At least, he would have been on guard duty had he actually been awake. Heaven only knew how he'd managed to drag that gut up two hundred stairs, Modeset reflected.

He crept over to the man, took a few moments to consider how his ancestors might have tackled the situation, and pummelled him on the head with the hilt of a dagger. Then, groaning with the effort, he dragged the unconscious figure away from the base of the ladder before beginning his ascent.

There were muffled voices coming from the other

side of the trapdoor. Raising it a gnat's wing, Modeset heard snatches of conversation.

'Won't stay still, Mistress!'

'Idiot! Just concentrate, will you?'

''Snot my fault, Mistress! The 'orrid little thing keeps running between the tubes! Maybe we should fetch the rest of them, and then—'

'Don't be ridiculous! If you can't keep one of them in check, how on Illmoor do you envisage handling six?'

'Well, I thought . . . er . . . can't we follow the prophecy with one lizard?'

'No! The machine must be at full strength, and that requires the glare of no less than six!'

'But Mistress, the intruders—'

'are pathetic incompetents. I can assure you, Edwy, I've dealt with the only one capable of any kind of offence. Now, just do as you're tol—'

Before the Lark could finish, the trapdoor flew open and Modeset erupted from within. Fuelled by an uncharacteristic taste for battle that went far beyond simple heroism, he pitched both daggers at Edwy and let out a scream of victory when one of them caught the Yowler disciple just above the kneecap. Edwy grabbed at his leg, gasped and fainted.

'You?' cried the Lark. 'Modeset, isn't it? The Great Duke of Rats! Hahahaha!' She took a step back while at the same time removing a glass sphere from the sleeve of her robe. Muttering incantations under her breath, she flung the sphere towards Modeset, eyes gleaming as it erupted into flame. The duke, still thinking on his feet, used the silver sabre to field it right back at her, his fist closed tightly around Bowlcock's fist on the handle.

The sphere exploded in the Lark's face with a subdued flare. As she staggered against the far wall, Modeset saw his chance and darted forward.

One thrust with the silver sabre shattered the huge glass eye of the lighthouse. It was only as Modeset turned to take out the glare machine that he realized his mistake. The Lark should have been his priority.

Now he found himself faced with the machine.

In the few seconds he'd taken to demolish the glass eye, Lauris had wheeled the machine around to face him. Somewhere in those tubular bowels, the Batchtiki was glaring. Its stare, reflected and magnified through a network of tiny mirrors, fired a ray directly at the duke.

This is it, he thought. I'm absolutely, positively, going to die.

He closed his eyes.

He swallowed.

He held his arms up over his head and crossed them.

Then it happened.

The Batchtiki's ray hit Modeset's shiny wrist guard and beamed back directly along its length. When the duke finally did pluck up enough courage to open his eyes, the machine had been turned to stone.

Silence reigned in the little room.

Modeset put a fingertip to his forehead and wiped away a bead of sweat.

'And let that be a lesson to you,' he said, and passed out.

The Lark screamed with fury, levitated off the floor and flew forward. She had almost reached Modeset's prone figure when a small fist like bunched metal slammed into her face.

Flicka stood over the duke, fists raised defensively. With the Lark still reeling from her blow, she executed a low kick into the priestess's stomach and brought up her other knee to finish the job.

The Lark hit the ground, somersaulted backwards and leapt to her feet again. Then she spun around with a backhand of her own and Flicka, caught unawares, tripped on Modeset's arm. She fell to the floor, gasping as her hand crunched awkwardly beneath her.

'Foolish girl,' spat the Lark, a second fire sphere already in her hands. She took aim, smiled grimly and released it.

Flicka rolled aside at the last minute, struggling to her feet as the sphere exploded mere inches from the duke's unconscious form. Then, muttering incantations under her breath, she raised both palms and sent two miniature bolts of lightning on a zigzag course towards the priestess.

Electricity filled the air and, for the briefest of seconds, it actually looked as if the Lark was in trouble. A wave of her hands quickly dispelled the illusion and she stood firm once again, shaken and bleeding, but still with all her wits about her.

'So . . . a fledgling sorceress,' she said. 'How . . . endearing. Your vampire offered no challenge, I wonder if you might?'

Without another word, she closed her eyes and levitated off the floor, arms held high and lips mouthing inaudible chants.

Flicka blinked, and swallowed. She knew a little magic, enough to keep the witches away from the Fogrise water supply when she was a child, but she'd never read much beyond chapter four of *Migellan's Mastery*. This woman, on the other hand, looked as if she might actually know what she was doing.

A large ruby red mist had begun to swirl around her, gathering pace as it developed into a swathe of cloud. The speed of the cloud intensified, swirling faster and faster until the Lark was nothing more than a shadow in the eye of the storm.

The room swam with magic.

The stone machine shattered.

Flicka prayed.

And Duke Modeset, having woken from his own self-enduced slumber, held aloft the silver sabre (arm and all) and hurled it with all his might at the centre of the cloud. Or else he would have done if his ancestor's appendage hadn't chosen that moment to take over.

The dead arm of Lord Bowlcock glowed a ghostly

green as it floated on the air, sabre raised high. Suddenly, it swung back and released the blade, which travelled at lightning speed across the room, spinning over and over on a fierce and unstoppable course.

There was a moment of silence in which the air tingled so loudly that it set the duke's teeth on edge.

Then the magic died, instantaneously.

The Lark, with blood leaking between her lips, staggered back with the sword protruding from her stomach.

'May the great Yowler curse you all in your graves,' she said, and died.

Flicka hurried over to the duke and flung her arms around him. Standing there, with his secretary's daughter clinging to him like a limpet, Modeset made a startling realization that this was infinitely more terrifying than the priestess *or* the narrowly averted destruction of Dullitch.

This, he thought, is the closest I've ever got to a real woman. A voice deep within his subconscious added: something you're definitely going to have to rectify.

Flicka peered up at him through tearful eyes.

'I have something to tell you, Lord M,' she said, snivelling.

'Go on.'

'It's about Obegarde; I'm afraid he's dead.'

$\mathcal{E}$leven

An interesting scene greeted Modeset and Flicka as they arrived on the landing below, dragging the unconscious form of Edwy after them.

They stopped in their tracks.

Jimmy Quickstint, looking dazed but aware, was standing over the trembling, obese guard that Modeset had encountered previously, the model blunderbuss pointed right at the disciple's groin.

'This is Moors,' he said. 'I think he wants to tell us a story.'

'P-p-please don't kill me!' the disciple gibbered. 'I don't know how I got involved in all of this! I only wanted to be part of something!'

Modeset glanced at Flicka and then stepped forward.

'Do you know how we can repair the damage your lunatic cult has caused?'

Moors shook his head, and blubbed.

'N-n-no,' he said.

'Then we're not interested in mercy,' continued the duke. 'Jimmy, pull the trigger.'

'NO! PLEASE! I'll tell you how to reverse the work of the glare machine.'

'And return everyone to their flesh state?'

'Yes.'

'How marvellous. And after that?'

Moors looked confused; sweat beaded on his brow.

'I don't follow?'

'Oh, you don't? Jimmy!'

The gravedigger raised the blunderbuss once more.

'OK, OK . . . what else do you want?'

'I want to know everything,' he said. 'From beginning to end, start to finish; the whole pathetic story. You can begin with the reversal procedure.'

It took a few minutes for Moors to stop snivelling. He plunged a hand into the pockets of the elephantine robe that draped his endless rolls of gut, and produced a small mirror on a chain.

'Mirrors,' he said weakly. 'If the Batchtiki glares in daylight, it turns flesh to stone. If its glare is reflected, stone becomes flesh. Or so the scripture says.'

'I find that hard to believe; my wrist guard reflected the lizard's stare directly. How come the lizard didn't turn to stone?'

'The Batchtiki are a species cursed by the gods.

They can't see themselves. Well-known fact.'

'Is it.'

'Y-yes. We had to reverse a few glares in our testing phase. You just point the lizard away from you, hold a mirror up to it and aim at whoever you want to be r-refreshed.'

Modeset nodded, and grabbed the chain.

'Very well,' he said, turning to Flicka. 'Take this and go downstairs to the room with the lizard cage. Change Pegrand back; be careful. When he's human again, or at least has returned to his usual state of equivalence, perform a similar ritual on the people of Plunge. Make sure they know what happened here, and who is responsible for saving them; namely us.'

Flicka frowned.

'You think they'll be grateful, Lord M?'

'No, but at least we won't get rocks thrown at us when we try to leave. Oh, and have Obegarde taken to the town chapel. We'll bury him here in Plunge; after all, he did try to save the place and I'm sure the people here will show him more respect than any Dullitch citizen could afford.'

Flicka started off down the spiral staircase, followed by Jimmy who was still wielding the blunderbuss as if he truly believed that a vivid imagination could fire the thing.

'Right,' said Modeset, turning with a snarl on the last remaining disciple. 'Do you know what this is?'

He brought an arm round from behind his back and brandished the silver sabre.

Moors shook his head; sweat was streaming down his cheeks.

'This,' the duke went on, 'spelled oblivion for your friend the Lark. Let us see what it spells for you.'

He lowered the sabre and allowed it to nudge the throat of Moors.

'Well?' he prompted. 'I think it wants to know everything almost as much as I do. You're not going to disappoint us both, surely?'

'N-n-no. I'll talk . . .'

'Yes, you will. Go on, then!'

'I worked at Counterfeit House. I was lonely; no wife, no kids and no friends? So I looked around for something to do, some kind of meeting I could go to.'

'A meeting for sad, lonely people?'

'Yes . . . you must know what I mean. I can smell fellow unfortunates a mile off.'

Modeset tried not to look uncomfortable and applied the merest fraction of pressure upon the sabre.

'Ahhh . . . all right! So anyway, I found this new group that had started up at the Yowler church. The regular worshippers got together on Friday nights, but I was always working then. The Holy Convocation of Lopsalm met of a Tuesday lunchtime.'

'So you went along?'

Moors nodded.

'The Lark was there, and Lopsalm. Mixer, the gnome, joined a few days after me; he was just a cleaner at the church, but they soon had him running round as an assassin. They chose him as the keeper of the great book, then faked a robbery so that the Yowler priests wouldn't get suspicious when it went missing. It was all the Lark's doing. She and Lopsalm were always conspiring, whispering to each other about some kind of deal they wouldn't let the rest of us in on.'

'The rest of you? You and Mixer, you mean.'

Moors wiped a globule of saliva from his fat lips.

'And Edwy,' he blubbed, pointing at the prone figure, 'he came last. He was workin' at the church as a caretaker, too. He'd overheard one of the meetings. They talked him into becoming number five.'

'I see.'

'And then, one night, they told us.'

Modeset raised an eyebrow.

'Told you? Told you what?'

'About the machines; that's what all the whisperin' had been about. They'd found this mad inventor who'd been thrown out of the Mechanics' Society. Somehow, between the three of them, they'd made exact replicas of the machines Doiley used in *Leaving Legends* to turn the people of Plunge to stone.'

'And you were shown these machines immediately?'

Moors nodded.

'Lopsalm assigned us each a task. I was in charge of

the reflecting machine, finding a place to hide it and then keeping it hidden. It wasn't too difficult; I used to be pretty influential in the guild. Edwy organized the church rota so that no one else found out about our Tuesday meetings. Mixer was supposed to tie up loose ends.'

'Such as?'

'The thief brought the lizards, so he had to go. The Lark had friends at Counterfeit House who sorted out a high-level forgery for her; they had to go. The old inventor . . . well, you get the picture.'

Modeset lowered the sabre slightly.

'The inventor was killed too?'

'Oh no,' said Moors, heaving a sigh of relief as the edge of the blade drew away. 'Mixer put the frighteners on the old fool, and we never saw him after that.'

'Who came up with the idea in the first place?'

'Lopsalm, but really the Lark triggered it all off. During her time at the palace, Mistress Lauris'd studied ancient lore. She discovered the Batchtiki, learned about their natural habitat. She even spent a few weeks in Grinswood checkin' up to see if the tomes were right. It was Lopsalm who suggested the theft; he's hated the dukes ever since he was fired from the palace.'

'What? *Lopsalm* worked for Curfew?'

'No,' said Moors. 'For Vitkins. That's where he met the Lark. Then Lord Vitkins died and you came in, your lordship. They disliked you right enough, but nothing like they hate your cousin. Oh, they *despised* Mr Curfew, said he wasn't a patch on either you *or* your uncle, said he'd bring the city down.'

'But the Yowlers put him in power!'

'They had to! He was your only relative: the main order wouldn't get rid of him because he was *of the blood*. That's when the group came up with this idea of breakin' away from the others 'n' turnin' everyone to stone. S'posed to bring back Yowler, it was. Ha! They must've been mad, believin' all that rubbish . . .'

'Yes,' said Modeset, thoughtfully. 'Religion has a lot to answer for.'

'It's not just that, Lord Modeset. *Nobody* likes Viscount Curfew. He's a spiteful man. Lopsalm thought the cult could make a difference, put him in his place.'

'By turning the population to stone?'

'It seemed like a good idea at the time; Lopsalm and the Lark made it all seem so . . . noble. I never meant to hurt anyone.'

'No, people like you seldom do. So, basically, Lopsalm and the Lark cooked this whole mess up between them, and you and your pathetic cohorts were merely pawns in their little game?'

Moors considered the question.

'Lopsalm's crazy,' he said eventually. 'I truly believe that. But the Lark, she knew what she was doing. I reckon she'd been planning to pull off something big for years. Fate probably brought the two of 'em together.'

'Hmm.'

Modeset stepped back.

'The people of Plunge will want an explanation,' he said. 'I'm sure that you'll be more than happy to provide them with one, after you've cleared up what little remains of your beloved mistress.'

He licked his lips, turned and headed off down the spiral staircase.

'And let this be a lesson to you,' he called back. 'Cults have a tendency to be dangerous and manipulative; so, next time you want friends, try joining something sensible . . . like the church.'

Twelve

Reanimating the people of Plunge turned out to be a tough (and largely thankless) task. Most of them had little or no idea of what had happened and therefore, upon regaining consciousness, quickly came to the inevitable conclusion that somebody had broken into their homes to point a lizard away from them. It was hard to fathom, and resentment was rife. Eventually, the mayor would explain at great length just how much in Modeset's debt they all were but, for the time being, chaos reigned.

Jareth Obegarde was carried to a plinth on the edge of the village where a small service was performed. The wound in his chest had closed and his eyelids twitched several times, but nobody seemed to notice.

The service itself was nothing to write home about, especially since the Plunge priesthood had only a vague notion of what a loftwing *was*. Instead, they resorted to the more usual speeches full of useful phrases like 'Rest in peace', 'Take it easy' and 'Don't get up for the milkman'.

Modeset was the only mourner who cried, although Pegrand wasn't entirely sure that it wasn't due to the bite of the wind.

As the small group made their way back down to the village, they were informed that a raven had arrived, heralding an important message from Dullitch.

Modeset read it through carefully and smiled.

'Those wishing to be teleported back to the city by the all-powerful hand of the grand Wrickshaw Muldoon must stand in the town square at noon tomorrow. The city will pay a small recompense for anyone who quickly forgets the use of magic involved in this procedure.'

'He must be quite the ticket, that wizard,' Pegrand said, taking the note when Modeset proffered it to him.

'Are you serious, man? You've seen him—'

'Yes, milord, but he *did* get us all out here in one piece . . . mostly. Besides, look, he's got letters after his name: G.O.F. What's that, Grand Order of—'

'It probably stands for Geriatric Old Fool. Now do get a move on. We need to find somewhere to stay tonight.'

Thirteen

The following evening, Modeset released a giant raven from the highest window of Plunge Keep. On reflection, he could've sent the note back with Jimmy, but teleportation spells were dicey at the best of times and he couldn't risk *this* note going astray.

'Nice of Baron Herpes to let us stay here, milord,' said Pegrand, straightening his jerkin in the chamber's angular mirror.

'It's Herps, Pegrand. Baron H-e-r-p-s. And we *did* save his subjects from being turned to stone.'

'Well, actually, milord—'

'Yes, OK, we didn't. Satisfied? But at the very least, we turned them from stone back into flesh. Surely that deserves food, board and lodgings for a couple of days. Besides, this was once part of my land;

that counts for something, doesn't it?'

'Of course, of course. So what was the raven's message about?'

'A message to Viscount Curfew telling him about the Lark, her group and the conclusion of this unholy mess.'

Pegrand nodded.

'Where's Flicka?' he asked, looking around.

'She teleported back to Dullitch with Jimmy,' Modeset said. 'She's going to pick up Vicious, the gods forbid, and Hopkirk, assuming he's willing to stay awake long enough to board a carriage. She will then accompany them back to Fogrise; the usual way. We're walking; it's safer and, besides, I've decided that we need the exercise. We should get to the border by noon.'

It took a few minutes for Modeset's meaning to dawn on Pegrand. When it did, the result wasn't pleasant.

'We're going home, milord?' he exclaimed. 'B-back to Fogrise?'

'Yes.'

'Do you think Earl Ripps'll give the kingdom back?'

'Not without a fight, old friend, not without a fight. I was thinking that perhaps we might whip the peasants into a frenzy – do you think they're the right sort for a revolt?'

'Dunno, milord. They're certainly revolting.'

Modeset patted his manservant companionably on the back.

'That's what I like about you, Pegrand. Your inimitable

sense of humour. Did you manage to return the sabre to the museum?' he asked.

'Yes, milord.'

'And you apologized for the mess?'

'Yes, milord.'

'And, of course, you helped clean up?'

'Absolutely, milord. I worked so fast, they couldn't see me for dust.'

'Hmm . . . I'm sure. Then we're almost ready to leave. I'm going to thank Baron Herps for his hospitality. Do get a move on, won't you?'

Pegrand waited until the sound of the duke's footsteps had dissipated, and raised a defiant middle finger.

Duke Modeset, crossing the boundary between Fogrise and Plunge, looked out across a hundred acres of swampland.

'Home is where the heart is, Pegrand,' he said. 'A pity we have to go back to Fogrise, instead.'

The manservant gave the question due consideration, and shrugged. He'd spent most of his life in the dreary little kingdom, and harboured no particular desire to return there.

'Can't we just skirt round it, milord? I'm sure you'd get a hero's welcome in Dullitch.'

Modeset looked incredulous.

'The people of Dullitch are fickle,' he exclaimed. 'Besides, Curfew will invariably hush up any talk of our escapades. In fact, I doubt very much if the people of Dullitch will ever know just how close to oblivion they were; Curfew certainly won't risk any wrath from the Yowlers. All that aside, I can't sit by and watch someone else run my city – it's not my way. I'd rather return to my beloved ancestral home at Fogrise.'

'You said you hated it, milord.'

'Well, yes . . . but—'

'You said you'd gladly sit back and watch it fall into the swamp.'

'Enough!'

Modeset's expression could've melted lead. Pegrand saw a fire in the duke's eyes that he hadn't glimpsed since the early days, when the kingdom still had a decent wall.

'We shall rebuild it,' Modeset said, his voice determined. 'Bigger, greater and grander than ever it was!'

'Won't be too difficult, milord,' said the manservant, on reflection. 'Hut with a turret should do it.'

'Did I already mention how much I hate you, Pegrand?'

'Frequently, milord. You old joker, you.'

Modeset looked up towards the heavens, and wondered if the gods were laughing.

Fourteen

The throne room at Dullitch Palace was enjoying the kind of silence that was merely a precursor to the inevitable din of someone losing their temper.

Viscount Curfew shuffled through a mountain of paperwork, gritted his teeth and then threw the whole pile into the air. As pieces of tattered parchment drifted to the ground all around him, he snatched two at random and tried to read both at the same time.

'None of this makes sense,' he groaned, glaring across the desk at Master Sorrow, who sat beside Jimmy Quickstint. 'I have different accounts of the same situation, and a letter from Modeset flatly contradicting everything else. You do realize that I'm going to have to employ somebody specifically to unravel all this mess, don't you?'

'Sorry about that, Sir,' said Sorrow. 'But it's a tricky situation. This is a very intricate case and these reports appear to have come at it from different angles.'

'Yes, I can see that,' agreed Curfew, scratching his fingernails over the rough wooden surface of his desk. 'The investigator, Obegarde, wasn't it? He caught the gnome?'

Sorrow nodded.

'Yes, Excellency.'

'The gnome who carried out at least one murder on the orders of a man called Lopsalm who you – Jimmy – witnessed commit suicide yesterday evening up at the cathedral.'

The gravedigger, who'd managed to shrug off his usual gawp in the presence of royalty, attempted to nod but only managed a small cough.

'And according to one of these unfathomable statements,' the viscount continued, 'Lopsalm was in league with a young lady who, it now seems obvious, was referred to as Lauris or the *Lark*. Correct?'

'Yes, Sir,' confirmed Sorrow. 'I read that somewhere in there, too.'

'Good; it would appear my delightful cousin has dealt with her.' He spent a few moments reorganizing the remaining papers on the desk before turning his attention back to the group.

'Let's see . . . Edwy, another member of this despicable order, and a man called Moors, are being brought up from Plunge for questioning? And we've also obtained a book from the gnome's hovel on Rump Lane. That, Mister Sorrow, would appear to be all she wrote.'

'*She*, Sir? There's a third witness?'

'An expression, Sorrow. Do not dwell on it.'

'Yes, Sir. No, Sir. Won't, Sir.'

'Good.'

'Can Mr Quickstint go now, Sir?'

Curfew nodded.

'You can show him out by all means. Just reward him and make sure he doesn't leave town, so to speak. We may need his help to further document this matter.'

'Yes, SA!'

Sorrow stood to attention, saluted and marched from the room without a second glance. After a few minutes he realized his mistake and returned to escort the witness away.

Curfew rolled his eyes, and prayed for the day when he wouldn't have to deal with such glaring ignorance.

Fifteen

Outside the palace, Jimmy Quickstint stood watching the moons. The gravedigger felt itchy with excitement; he'd certainly had an extraordinary week. However, the sight of his old boss leaving the Dog and Duck did a lot to bring him crashing back to earth.

'Evenin', Mr, er, Coldwell,' he ventured, praying desperately that he'd remembered the old man's name correctly.

'Evenin'.'

'Nice night, Sir.'

'Aye,' came the expected reply.

'Busy up at the cemetery, I'll bet?'

'Aye.'

'Got another assistant yet, have you?'

'Nope.'

'Lookin' for one?'

'Aye.'

'I don't suppose there's any chance . . .'

The old man flicked his flat cap with a grimy forefinger.

'Aye.'

'I'll want better conditions, though.'

' 's tha' right?' The old man swung his shovel over one shoulder, raised a bushy eyebrow. 'An' what'd those be?'

'Um . . . an extra crown an hour.'

'Aye.'

'More help when I'm digging.'

'How d'you mean, like?'

'Well, you could at least hold the lantern or something.'

'Aye, ahright. That all?'

Jimmy considered all his demands.

'Yes,' he said finally. 'Well, also, I'd like to know who's sharing with my uncle.'

Sixteen

It was early evening in Plunge, and rain poured in torrents over the sleepy town. In the makeshift graveyard which surrounded a solitary chapel on the cliff top, a gravestone toppled backwards, slamming into the grass with a cushioned thud. A few inches from the upturned base, a fist erupted through the turf, straightened into a hand and felt around a bit. Then it disappeared.

A voice from within said: 'At least the sun's not out; that's something.'

A few moments passed as the rain diminished into a fine mist.

Then the ground imploded, grass and mud spewing into the grave as Obegarde frantically clawed his way out. The loftwing, bare-chested but still clad in his trademark raincoat, rolled on to his back and took a deep gulping breath while the fine rain soaked into his flesh.

Nearby, a squirrel stopped assaulting a nut to watch him quizzically. Obegarde struggled up on to his elbows, and grimaced when he saw the little creature observing him.

At the other end of the graveyard, an old lady tending a tiny grave beside the gates had frozen to the spot with fear. As Obegarde made his way past, he smiled at her.

'Nice day we're having, ma'am. Looks like I'm the first one up. Well, see you around.'

The old woman's bottom lip quivered, and she forced herself to watch the stranger as he made his way down the road towards Plunge's town square. After a time, she turned back to her husband's grave.

'Henry,' she said, hopefully. 'Do you know that man?'

THE END

Thanks to:

My mother, Barbara Ann Stone, who watched me craft this book and prizes it above all others. My girlfriend, Chiara Louisa Tripodi, the rock of support to which I regularly anchor. Thanks also to Bob Lea, the illustrator who puts 'em all to shame, Anne McNeil, who's lived in Illmoor almost as long as I have, and Joanna Solomon, who ably assists her. Finally, I must mention the legendary Irish comedian, Dave Allen, my first inspiration in the world of comedy writing. From the age of eight I listened to Dave describing life in his own inimitable style: nobody did it better. Dave, I'm glad you're still at large – this one's for you! (I'd also like to thank Susan Williams, for obtaining Dave's permission to mention him here!)